IMPLICATION

Gripping crime fiction with a cruel twist

RAY CLARK

Published by The Book Folks

London, 2022

This book is a work of fiction. Names, characters, businesses, organizations, places and events are either the product of the author's imagination or are used fictitiously. Any resemblance to actual persons, living or dead, events or locales is entirely coincidental.

ISBN 978-1-80462-044-1

www.thebookfolks.com

IMPLICATION is the ninth book in a series of mysteries by Ray Clark featuring DI Stewart Gardener. The full list of books is as follows:

1. IMPURITY

2. IMPERFECTION

3. IMPLANT

4. IMPRESSION

5. IMPOSITION

6. IMPOSTURE

7. IMPASSIVE

8. IMPIOUS

9. IMPLICATION

***Implication:* 1.** *What is involved in or implied by something else.* **2.** *The act of implicating or implying.* **3.** *By what is implied or suggested rather than by formal expression.*

"When I consider life, 'tis all a cheat;
Yet fooled with hope, men favour the deceit."

John Dryden

Chapter One

Dominic Appleby could count on the fingers of one hand the things in life that pleased him at that moment, and he still wouldn't reach all five digits.

Dressed in fashionable, bright orange running gear with black trainers, he turned and closed the front door of the bungalow. Reaching into his pocket he grabbed the mini headphones, plugged the jack into his phone, the buds into his ears, found his music and pressed play.

As Survivor's *Eye of the Tiger* cranked up, he headed down the drive and turned right on to Haygate Lane in Bursley Bridge. He glanced upwards at a bright blue sky and set off into a steady jog, as had been his routine for the last three years since buying the place.

Appleby was not a fan of old music. Give him modern artists any day of the week – Jack Savoretti, Lewis Capaldi, Adele, to name but a few. But he had always felt the Survivor track was the perfect opening piece to set the pace.

Despite hitting a steady rhythm almost instantly, he found himself immediately distracted by the state of not only his life, or the country, but the entire world if he was being honest.

He'd heard enough about the pandemic to last him a lifetime – hadn't everyone? Thanks to the media ranting on about it every single day. What they didn't know they would make up. *Did anyone actually believe the statistics they were coming out with?* If they could possibly find a new angle with which to frighten everyone to death, they would.

If that wasn't bad enough, they created panic-buying with their ridiculous headlines and stories – the last one being the fuel crisis. Two fuel stations had run out. They reported it along with some other hype – next thing you knew, we really *were* running out.

Appleby felt himself pounding the ground harder in an effort to release the frustration, instead of actually enjoying the fresh country air and views.

The music changed but Appleby barely realized it as his thoughts had now turned to a government that were as incompetent as the media; a bunch of clowns, with the ringmaster proving worse than the rest of them. Appleby grimaced when he thought of how the man dressed like a tramp, acted like a court jester and flatly refused to answer any question unless it was about the vaccine rollout. It was history. Move on. Address the real problems.

Appleby earned his living through stock and shares, which had been performing abysmally of late. The interest rates had slipped out of sight, although that finally appeared to be changing. Energy prices were going through the roof. He didn't even want to think about Russia.

He suddenly remembered something from his childhood. When he was about ten years old, his dad had dragged him to see The Hollies in concert. He remembered a comment the lead singer had made about how things were so bad in Britain that he was down to his last Rolls Royce, and even had to borrow stage clothes from Donny Osmond – maybe he should try living here now.

Appleby had reached the intersection quicker than he realized. Haygate Lane bore off to the right, but he took the left fork down East Ings Lane, which was a dead-end road that lead to a scrapyard.

He slowed as he reached a gate on his left. Still running on the spot, he reached into his pockets and extracted a couple of carrots, and called out to the horses in the field. They were already out of their stables and waiting at the gate; everyone knew the routine. He fed them a carrot each and continued on his way.

As he set off, the music changed again to one of Adele's big hits. His phone bleeped. Reaching down, he pulled it out of his pocket and stared at the screen, no mean feat while you were running. The text was from Claire, his latest girlfriend, hoping to arrange something for the weekend. He would message her later, after his run.

He liked Claire. They had been dating for six months and complemented each other very well, with similar tastes in music, food, films, sport, and a great many other things.

Appleby suddenly became aware of a strange odour, one he couldn't quite place, but it smelled a bit like a barbeque. Though why anyone would be cooking food outside on a grille at six o'clock on a March morning no matter how nice the weather, was beyond him. But it took all sorts.

Another text suddenly brought his attention to a share price that had rapidly declined as the markets closed the previous evening. He'd invested in a foreign digital media company about a year ago when the shares were next to nothing. Six months in, they had tripled. Now they were almost back to their starting price. He should have sold when he'd had the chance.

He would give it some thought. Though the markets were traditionally closed on weekends, Dominic was known as a swing trader. That meant he still played them, favouring a modern option order flow platform called CheddarFlow. CF tracked the purchase of either call or put options, betting on the stock price going up or down.

He put the phone back in his pocket and caught the strange odour again. It appeared closer if that was possible. On his right were open fields. To his left, he could neither see through, nor past, the tall hedge. As he removed his headphones, he became aware of a crackling sound, like that of a fire.

He ran about twenty yards further where there was another gate. The crackling grew louder, the smell stronger, and at that point he became aware of black smoke.

He reached the gate, stared into the field, and was shocked to see a large van merrily burning away.

He grabbed his phone.

Chapter Two

Less than ten minutes after the call had come in, Chief Fire Officer Liam Seddon was sitting in the passenger seat of the fire engine as it approached the field. He had his hand on the door handle and as soon as the big vehicle shuddered to a halt, he jumped out.

Checking behind the engine, he saw the police panda had pulled up as well. PC Mike Atherton exited the car.

"Is this it?"

Seddon nodded. He knew Atherton quite well. He was twenty-six, married with two young children and had transferred to Bursley Bridge a year or so back from a station in Suffolk. Atherton was tall, had short dark hair, and a serious expression. But he was dedicated and easy to work with.

Seddon turned and approached the gate, passing a man dressed in sportswear, whom he suspected had probably made the call. He would leave him to Atherton. Seddon's problem was the burning van. He stared upwards, thanking the Lord for a really clear day with no wind. He needed to follow National Operational Guidance as quickly as possible: the first thing to do would be to carry out a dynamic risk assessment to see how safe it was to approach the vehicle.

It was less than twenty meters in from the road, which made things easier. Seddon scurried toward the burning van with caution, quickly studying it from all angles. In his opinion, the fire had not been going long but could still do some serious damage if it reached the fuel tank in time. It appeared as if it had been started at the rear of the vehicle, and the flames were currently heading toward the middle. Glancing behind the passenger door he could see the panel that covered the fuel filler neck.

He came back around the side of the van and noticed two firefighters in full PPE, with gloves, flash hoods, and helmets with torches in. As it was less than sixty metres away from their vehicle, they could use the hose reel from the engine itself.

Atherton was talking to the man in the running gear.

Chris Meadows, one of the firefighters drew closer.

"Is it safe to approach?"

Behind Seddon, the burning vehicle crackled. Time was of the essence.

"Yes," he replied, "but keep your distance and for Christ's sake be ready at all times for any explosions."

He stepped back and allowed them to do their job. They quickly extinguished the fire using water, and when they were satisfied that all was safe, they stepped back nodding to Seddon.

Whilst the vehicle was cooling, Seddon took a thermal image of the scene in order to determine if anyone was lying around that could have been thrown from the wreckage of the van. He scanned the area through three hundred and sixty degrees, twice. Only when he was happy did he put the camera down and approach the front of the vehicle, which he could now see was a Ford Transit.

Meadows joined him.

"I'm going to have a look inside," said Seddon, "see what we might be dealing with. Can you disconnect the battery?"

Meadows nodded.

Seddon opened the driver's door and immediately felt under the steering wheel, pulling on the release handle for the bonnet. The cab was empty but the van was boarded out so he would need to open the back doors as well.

Slipping around the rear, Atherton approached him.

"See anything?"

"Not yet," replied Seddon.

"Can I join you?"

"Let me look in the back first; just to make sure there's nothing in there that's going to blow us all to pieces?"

Atherton appeared a little impatient. "Surely it would have done so by now."

"Depends what's in there, Mike. I was called to one scene a few years ago when both the fire chief and the PC attending thought the same thing. One of them opened the back doors and whatever was inside blew them both thirty feet in the air. Neither one survived. You've got kids, mate, I don't want to be the one telling them you're not coming home."

"So have you."

"Mine are older," countered Seddon, smiling. "Besides, it's my job."

Atherton nodded. "Be my guest."

Meadows suddenly appeared from the front of the vehicle. As he joined Seddon he said, "All safe, sir."

"Thanks, Chris."

"Are you doing the honours?" asked Meadows, staring at the rear doors, "or shall I?"

"Needs to be me, my friend. It's pretty much my name on the door."

Seddon stepped forward and tried the back doors, but for some reason they were jammed.

"Are they locked?" asked Meadows.

"I don't think so, probably the heat from the fire has warped them. Can you get me a crowbar?"

Meadows slipped back to the engine but promptly returned. Seddon took the bar and set about the doors. The vehicle cracked loudly as it cooled, spooking them both. Within a minute, Seddon had the doors open but he was far from happy with the contents of the van. He called Atherton over, whose eyes widened immediately. He reached for his mobile, calling Cragg back at the station.

It was beyond his remit. They needed MIT, the Major Investigation Team from Leeds Central.

Chapter Three

Within an hour of the call to Leeds Central, Detective Inspector Stewart Gardener and Detective Sergeant Sean Reilly pulled up in a pool car. Reilly parked behind the local panda car and the pair of them jumped out.

As he walked past the engine, Gardener, the SIO, nodded to Atherton, who was standing next to a man wearing running gear. Peering into the field, he noticed three fire officers. A fourth stood at the other side of the engine, smoking.

Gardener and Reilly approached PC Atherton and the SIO tipped his hat and extended his hand to shake.

"Good to see you again."

Atherton said likewise. Their last meeting had been when Gardener and his team were investigating a disreputable, almost invisible character by the name of Robbie Carter.

"What do we have, Mike?" asked Reilly.

Atherton pointed to the man in the running clothes. "This is Dominic Appleby, sir."

Appleby appeared to be in his early thirties. He had blond hair with a slim build that complemented the running gear. He had blue eyes and a five o'clock shadow.

"He left his house this morning shortly after six o'clock for a jog. Within a few minutes he came across this." Atherton pointed to the now charred van. "He called the brigade, who called us. Once the fire was out and we checked the van, we found a body inside."

"Oh, dear," said Gardener, introducing himself and Reilly to Appleby. "Not the best way to start your morning."

"No, but it was better than how he started his," replied Appleby, nodding towards the van.

"So you were jogging for about fifteen minutes and came across the burning van," said Gardener. "Did you see anyone else around, Mr Appleby?"

"No. I'm out most mornings but I never do see anyone – too early."

Gardener studied the area. It was pretty bleak with very little in the way of houses, though he figured there might be a farm or two because he'd noticed stables on the way up the lane, with a couple of horses in the field.

"You didn't see anyone when you came across the burning van?" asked Reilly. "Nothing out of the corner of your eye that might not have made sense at the time?"

Appleby's eyes moved left and right, and his serious expression deepened.

"Sorry, no. I think I was a bit too shocked."

"Understandable," said Gardener. "Did you call it in straight away?"

"Yes," said Appleby.

Gardener concluded there was nothing more he could gain from the conversation at that moment. He passed over a card and asked Appleby to call him if he remembered anything. He also asked Atherton to make sure someone called on Appleby to take a full and signed statement.

Gardener nodded and left them. He and Reilly slipped through the gate into the field. The fire chief stepped forward and introduced himself, taking them through what had happened since he'd arrived.

Seddon was dressed in full hi-vis clothing with sturdy boots. He was well built, slightly taller than Gardener at around six feet five, with a rough complexion, which Gardener suspected had a lot to do with his job, the hours he kept and the things he had to deal with.

"Is the vehicle safe?" asked Gardener.

"Yes," replied Seddon. "No dangerous chemicals inside. Might be some diesel left in the tank but there's nothing to worry about."

"Can we see the body?" asked Reilly.

"Yes."

Seddon led them over. Gardener glanced in through the open back doors. The scene made for interesting viewing. The van had been boarded out and most of the wood had now turned to charcoal, the smell quite overpowering.

For Gardener, the really interesting object was the shotgun, positioned at the front end of the vehicle. Like everything else, it had been affected by the fire but there was no mistaking what it was.

"Interesting, Sean," said Gardener.

"Wonder if the gun's been used, and what on," said Reilly, studying the body, which was in the foetal position. "Was he dead before the fire was started?"

Gardener leaned in closer, trying to examine as best he could without touching anything. Most of the clothing had burned away, leaving exposed and charred skin. The smell of charcoaled meat was present. The skin on the head had mostly been stripped.

"From the position, I'd guess so. That body isn't showing any signs of a struggle to escape the flames."

"Even if the van hadn't been burning long, the temperature would have been enough for him to create a commotion," added Reilly.

Gardener glanced over at Appleby and Atherton.

"I must remember to ask Appleby if he actually heard anything." He turned back to the interior of the van. "I know we have a gun but this doesn't look like suicide."

Reilly also leaned in closer. "No evidence of that, boss. If you're going to kill yourself with a gun, the first place you'd likely put it is inside your mouth – if you're serious." He pointed to the gun. "That there is a sawn-off shotgun, it would have made a right mess of him and most of the inside of the van."

"Apart from that, he wouldn't be laid as if he was sleeping," said Gardener. "Someone's staged this. He's been killed and put there and then the van set on fire, possibly as a way of disguising something else."

"Why the gun?" asked Reilly.

"A warning, maybe?" offered Gardener. "Perhaps they're trying to tell us something. It's obvious we'd be involved once it was found."

Also inside the van, between the body and the gun, there appeared to be a couple of electrical items, possibly laptops or iPads. Both had suffered severely from fire damage, and Gardener thought they would be very lucky to drag any information out of them – but it was always possible.

"You don't recognise him, do you?" Gardener asked of Seddon.

"Sorry, no – there isn't much *to* recognise, really."

Gardener hoped the man was local otherwise there was no telling where the investigation would lead them, or how long it would take. He stepped back and stared at the rear of the van. He couldn't see any number plates. He suspected someone had removed them prior to burning.

He turned to his partner. "Going to be a tough one."

Reilly nodded and smiled.

"They're all tough. Somebody obviously knew what they were doing here. He was dead before the fire was set, whatever is on those laptops will have gone, and the plates from the van are missing. A professional job?"

"That's what I was thinking, but there are other ways of identifying the van, so maybe we'll see it's not the job we thought," said Gardener.

"Doctor Death's going to love us, calling him out at this time," said Reilly. "Probably isn't even in his coffin yet."

"You will be if he hears you call him that," said Gardener, turning his attention to Seddon. "Doesn't look like it's been on fire long."

"Probably not," Seddon said. "Half an hour at the most before the jogger found it. When you start investigating you might want to concentrate on whatever accelerant has been used."

"How so?" Gardener asked.

"Every petrol station has underground tanks to store their fuel," replied Seddon. "Each tank degrades at a different rate, putting a small quantity of particles into the petrol in tiny amounts, which results in every station having its own chemical signature."

"Really?" said Gardener, learning something new.

"Arson is often solved by examining the chemistry of the petrol and matching it to the station. Once you have the station, that might give you guys a chance to grab the CCTV and credit card details of the buyer. Your arson investigator will no doubt have something locally referred to as 'the sniffer' – a clever little machine that detects the type of accelerant used to create the fire, and he can take it from there. After that, it should be straightforward."

"Thank you," said Gardener, noticing Reilly taking notes.

"No problem," replied Seddon. "I think we're about done here but if you need anything else, here's my card."

Gardener took it, put it in his pocket and tipped his hat before turning to Reilly.

"So, what have we got?" said Gardener. "Three scenes: the body itself, the van, and the place it was found."

"Pity the plates have gone," said Reilly. "Would have been nice if those had been in place, but never mind." He studied the open fields. "I can't see house-to-house revealing much. There aren't any nearby."

Gardener checked his watch. "I don't think there is much we can do here. I've called out the usual suspects: Fitz, the SOCOs, and PolSA – Police Search Advisors. We'll need them to conduct a fingertip search but even that might be asking a lot."

He glanced over at Atherton and then back to his partner.

"Can you ask him to lock it down with an inner and outer cordon? He might need some more of the officers from Bramfield. I'll ask our team to go straight to the station before coming here. We can brief them there and get them straight on with some tasks. I'll call Maurice Cragg and ask him to set up an incident room."

"We'll need an authorised garage to collect the van once we've finished with the scene," said Reilly. "They can stick it in a bay, and we can get a better look at it."

Gardener nodded before turning his attention rear to the van, staring inside once more. He had a bad feeling.

Chapter Four

Back outside the gate, Gardener wanted another word with Dominic Appleby, who was still where Atherton had left him. The Bramfield PC was standing near his own car, on his mobile – probably arranging back-up.

"Mr Appleby, can I have another quick word, please?"

"Of course." He stood around uneasily. "I wasn't sure if I was allowed to go back home so I was waiting until someone told me."

"Thank you," said Gardener. "What do you do for a living?"

"Stocks and shares."

"Would it be fair to assume you work from home?"

"Mostly."

Gardener nodded. Reilly joined them both as Gardener continued.

"Can I take you back to the van and when you first found it? I'm sure you'd have told me already, but I just need to clarify something. When you ran up towards this area, did you hear anything coming from the inside of the van? Any banging, or shouting?"

Appleby appeared to think deeply, frowning.

"No. I had my headphones on when I first came across it, but I imagine it wouldn't have mattered. I'm sure he would have made enough noise to wake the dead." Appleby paused. "I've been standing here thinking about it. Christ, it must have been awful, trapped in there with all that heat and smoke, knowing you were going to die. Who would do such a thing?"

Gardener glanced around, noticing more people attending the scene, but none of them were his team, which made him wonder where they had all come from.

He turned back to Appleby. "Sadly, that's where we come in. We have to find out."

"I wouldn't like your job."

"We don't, most of the time," said Reilly.

An Isuzu pick-up pulled up behind Atherton's police car, and a portly gentleman wearing a straw hat forced himself out.

"Okay, Mr Appleby, thank you for your time," said Gardener. "If you're staying at home today you might receive a visit from one of our team just to take an official statement."

Appleby nodded. "Am I okay… to go now?"

"Yes," said Gardener.

As Appleby left, the portly gentleman approached. He was wearing a tweed jacket, dungarees that were forced into submission but managing to hold everything together with a strong pair of braces, and Wellington boots. His complexion was red and ruddy, as if his face had been set on fire and put out with a shovel. All his teeth were there but they were uneven and discoloured, and he certainly didn't appear to have missed many meals.

"What's going on here, then?" he asked, his Yorkshire accent deep and blunt.

Gardener introduced himself and Reilly, before inquiring who *he* was.

"Bob North, farmer and owner of this here field."

Gardener explained what had happened, pointing to the charred van.

"Oh, dear me," said North. "How awful. Wouldn't like to think I'd finish my days like that."

Gardener doubted that would happen; they'd have to build the van around him. "You're not currently renting the field out to anyone, are you, Mr North?"

"No, sir. In fact I was planning on moving the sheep in here for grazing. I expect I won't be able to do that for a while."

"Hopefully, it won't be too long," said Gardener. "We'll try not to inconvenience you any more than necessary."

"Don't you worry about that none, sir," said North, tipping his hat. "You've got a rotten job to do and I know you need time to do it." The farmer turned and pointed down the lane, past the panda car and his own vehicle. "About a mile down there you'll see a field with stables, and a right turn just after it. Me and the wife and family all live there. You need anything, you just knock on my door."

"Thank you," said Gardener.

"What time were you up this morning, Bob?" asked Reilly.

"Bloody early, sir. About four, for the milking, like every morning."

"You didn't notice any activity?" asked Reilly. "Vans or cars, up and down the lane?"

"No, sir. It's not usual at that time. We live out in the sticks here and most of the businesses are farms, but we're about the only one down here. There's a few houses, and if you continue on down there" – he pointed the opposite way – "to East Ings Lane, it's a dead end, but there is a scrapyard at the bottom, run by a bloke called Mitchell. Dare say he might be of some help."

Gardener thanked him and said they would send someone round later for a statement. As North left, Gardener turned to face East Ings Lane then flinched and stepped back when he noticed that something resembling the Hunchback of Notre Dame had suddenly appeared from nowhere, standing near the gate, staring into the field.

"Feck me," said Reilly, also moving back.

The man had basically gone to seed. He was even more rotund than the farmer. He wore a woolly hat and Gardener noticed a thatch of thick grey hair sprouting out from underneath, heading in every direction – some of it even poked through the hat, as if he'd never removed it.

His attire was jeans, rigger boots, a check shirt, and a black body-warmer, most of which was stained with everything known to man, and a lot that was probably unknown. He had a round, wrinkleless face. As his mouth was open, catching flies, Gardener noticed the man's brown teeth perched inside like uneven tent pegs.

The SIO crept forward, introducing both himself and Reilly. He asked the man his name.

He appeared at first to not want to speak. In fact he actually peered around in an effort to ascertain whether or not it was him they were talking to.

"Who, me?"

Gardener momentarily stepped back. Whatever came out of his mouth smelled worse than the van and its contents.

"You see anyone else?" asked Reilly.

"Him." The man pointed to Atherton.

"He's twenty feet away," said Reilly. "We'd hardly be asking him anything at this distance. Besides, he's one of us."

Nothing further was said, so Gardener reminded him of the question.

"Frankie," he eventually said.

"Frankie what?" asked Reilly.

"Just Frankie."

Figuring that's all that was on offer, Gardener asked, "Where do you live, Frankie?"

"I haven't done anything."

Gardener was suddenly reminded of the *Two Ronnies* sketch, where Corbett asked Barker a question, and he answered the next question rather than the current one.

"Frankie," said Reilly, "I'm really not sure you have the hang of this. We ask you a question and you answer it. We don't need you to go all random on us. So, shall we try again, where do you live?"

Frankie pointed. "Down there."

Reilly followed his line of vision. "What – the field, a shed, a lay-by?"

"The scrapyard."

"You've done it again, haven't you?" said Reilly. "Okay, where do you live, and where do you work?"

"Scrapyard," said Frankie.

Gardener had better things to do than work out how far down the food chain he needed to go to communicate with the man, so he quickly changed topics.

"Have you seen any unusual activity this morning, Frankie?"

"Should I have?"

"That's what we'd like to know," said Reilly.

"Unusual?" repeated Frankie.

Reilly pointed toward the field. "Regarding that van."

Frankie then stared in all directions but the field, before eventually saying he hadn't.

"Have you seen anything at all unusual in the last few days?" asked Gardener. "Anything regarding vans coming up and down the lane at odd times, vans you don't recognise?"

Frankie sighed heavily. "I don't see much. It doesn't pay to see things."

Gardener didn't doubt any of what he'd said, but he wondered how much Frankie didn't see because he didn't want to.

"Okay, Frankie," said Gardener, "will you be going back to work now?"

"Expect so."

Frankie thrust a finger that resembled a carrot, into his mouth, and chewed on a nail, which was no mean feat with his teeth.

At that point, a number of vehicles appeared, parking up behind Atherton's car and the pool car, blocking off Haygate Lane. Two were Transit vans containing the SOCOs and PolSA. The Home Office pathologist, George Fitzgerald – otherwise known as Fitz – was in a car behind them.

Against his better judgment, Gardener passed Frankie a card.

"We'll be calling by the scrapyard later today, Frankie, to have a talk with you and Mr Mitchell. Can you tell him, please?"

Frankie stared at Gardener. "Tell him what?"

"That we're paying you a visit," said Reilly, careful not to lean in too close.

Frankie took the card and sighed, heavily. "He won't like that."

"I doubt we will," whispered Reilly.

"I appreciate that," said Gardener, "but I'm afraid we have a job to do and we'll be questioning everyone in the area."

"About what?" asked Frankie.

Reilly patted Frankie on the back. "We'll see you later, Frankie. Don't you worry yourself none."

As they turned, the SOCOs were standing by the gate, along with PolSA. Gardener and Reilly nodded and spoke to them, before stepping into the field with Fitz.

"How bad is it?" Fitz asked Gardener.

"We were hoping *you* might give *us* an idea."

All three men stared into the van. Fitz put his case on the ground and leaned inwards, examining as much as he could.

"The only thing I'm really interested in at the moment is the position of the body. If he was dead prior to burning, the remains would be still in the position they were left in."

"That's what we thought," said Reilly.

"If he'd been alive and awakened on burning," said Fitz, "his body position would show signs of distress, or at the very least, a struggle to escape the flames. I don't see any of that here, gentlemen, so I think it's safe to assume that this man was dead before the fire started."

"Which begs the question, dead how?" asked Gardener.

"Doesn't look like the shotgun had anything to do with it, but I'll be able to tell you more when I get him back to the mortuary."

"Will you be able to get anything from the body now that it's been burned?" asked Reilly.

Fitz studied the corpse again. "If the degree of burning is fairly slight – and it's hard to say with this one, as I can't see all of it – blood samples might still show any poison or drugs."

"If not?" asked Gardener.

"Well," said Fitz, "if it's badly burned, all traces of chemicals would probably disappear. A gunshot or stab wound will possibly leave a sign on a bone, which we will discover once he's on the slab, even on a badly burned body."

Fitz studied the inside of the van again.

"What are you looking for?" asked Gardener.

"Ropes or restraints," replied Fitz, "which would possibly leave a residue in the area where they were fastened. But, as you can see, gentlemen, there are none."

"Which compounds the theory that he was dead before the van was set on fire," added Gardener.

Chapter Five

Later that day, Reilly pulled the pool car to a halt outside the small country police station.

The large building resembled a town hall, with four steps leading to the front door, flanked either side by Grecian pillars and castellated mock battlements. Above the front door was a wrought-iron canopy with potted plants. The window frames were wooden; the exterior surrounded by lamps with gas mantles.

Both officers left the car and climbed the steps to the entrance. Gardener stopped and glanced around. The market town was busy with people milling around, going about their daily business, totally unaware of what he and Reilly had discovered. The cafés were busy and people sat outside because of the good weather.

"Feels like we've come home," said Reilly.

"That's just what I thought when you drove up," said Gardener.

"I've grown attached to the place," said Reilly, "despite what we end up finding."

Gardener nodded and smiled. However small the community was, it certainly held its fair share of dangerous people.

The SIO turned and strolled in through the front door. The lobby was spacious, with a counter along the back wall. At the moment the hatch was in the up position. To his left, Gardener noticed a cleaner at work, rearranging plant pots – a duster in one hand, the vacuum cleaner behind her. He then heard the familiar voice of the resident desk sergeant who had perhaps been here since the days of Sherlock Holmes.

"Good to see you again, sir," said Maurice Cragg, nodding and smiling. "Mr Reilly."

The pair of them strolled forward, toward the back room, the one that resembled someone's sitting room, with a table and chairs, a three-piece suite, a TV, a wooden floor with an assortment of rugs, and wallpaper from the 1950s.

Nothing ever changed in Bramfield.

"Take a seat, gentlemen. Kettle's boiled, tea's ready. One of the lads has been to the bakery in the town and we have a breakfast selection for you to choose from."

"I've decided when this case is over, I'm not leaving here," said Reilly.

"You might have to, sir," said Cragg. "We couldn't afford to feed you."

Gardener smiled. "The service *is* good."

Cragg sat down after he'd poured the tea and placed it on the table.

"Mike Atherton's updated me on the scene. Have we identified the body?"

"I'm afraid not," said Gardener.

In between eating a granola yoghurt pot, he filled Cragg in on all the details that he and Reilly were piecing together.

"Could be a nasty one, this," said Cragg. "Anyway, we have a room set up and most of your team are here. I've only explained bits to them, but I'll come and join you once you get started."

After refreshments, Gardener and Reilly found the team in one of the downstairs rooms. Inside the room were a number of tables and chairs, tea and coffee facilities, a variety of pads and pens, and two whiteboards, which at the moment were empty. Hopefully before close of play they would be covered with photographs.

Gardener took to the front, welcoming the team, explaining that DS Bob Anderson and DS Frank Thornton were in their final day of self-isolating due to Covid, but they were okay and should be able to join them tomorrow.

With Reilly's help, he then explained everything they knew, which wasn't much. Where to go from here would prove interesting.

Before Gardener started issuing actions, Cragg slipped into the room and took a seat. As usual, his arms were full of paraphernalia that would probably be of the utmost importance to them.

PCs Paul Benson and Patrick Edwards were sitting together toward the back of the room.

"Patrick, Paul, I think I'll start you on house-to-house. It's not going to be easy, there are only a few and they're well spaced out."

"This might help, sir," said Cragg. "It's a local map of the area, shows all the houses and farms."

Gardener's mind went to the farmer they met earlier, Bob North, and he requested that Benson and Edwards specifically pay him a visit. He also mentioned Dominic Appleby and the need for a signed statement, and as they were in the vicinity, they would have an opportunity to view the scene itself.

"Try to cover as much of the area as you can around East Ings Lane and Haygate Lane," said Gardener, "but you can leave the scrapyard to us."

"We've already had first-hand experience of the hobbit that works there," said Reilly.

"Bad as that, is he?" said Benson.

"You don't know the half of it," said Reilly. "We asked where he worked and lived, and he gave us the same answer for both questions – the scrapyard."

"Doesn't he speak English?" asked Benson.

"In a fashion," said Reilly. "Not sure he actually understands it."

"Put it this way," added Gardener, "we wouldn't wish him on anyone."

"Think we'll be quite happy to leave that to you, sir," said Edwards, studying the map Cragg had given him.

"I take it you're talking about Frankie," said Cragg. "He's definitely a sandwich short of a picnic."

"More than one if you ask me," said Reilly.

"Do you know anything about him?" Gardener asked Cragg.

"Surprisingly, no," said Cragg. "He appeared to drift into town with a bad storm one night. Storm left but he didn't. No history to speak of. He's a bit of a drinker and a gambler from all accounts, but I don't think he's ever been in front of us for anything. Rumour has it that one night, after running out of alcohol, egged on by the card school he was playing with, Frankie tried a glass of battery acid, the result of which melted his teeth."

The team broke down in tears of laughter and DC Dave Rawson shouted, "Oh, come on, sir, you have to give him to us. I'd love to see this bloke."

Gardener had found it funny but continued assigning actions to the team.

"Van identification will be high on the list. I'd like the girls to tackle this one. Once the scene is released the van will be towed to an authorized garage." The SIO glanced at Cragg. "Will that be here in Bramfield, Maurice?"

"I don't think so, sir," replied Cragg. "I think it's best if it goes to the nearest Ford dealer, which is probably York."

"I take it, it's a Transit, then?" asked PC Julie Longstaff.

Gardener nodded.

"Without plates?" asked DS Sarah Gates. "I assume they're either burned off or missing."

"Missing," replied Gardener, "but there are a number of things we can have a look at that will help us. I did take the liberty of calling the Ford dealer in York to ask about how we would identify it. They asked for a picture of the van and from that they worked out that it would have been manufactured between 2010 and 2014. The big thing to watch out for here is that the chassis number – which is our best chance of identification – is located in three different places."

"It's either on a plate under the bonnet on the slam panel, or on the bulkhead at the back of the engine bay," Reilly said. "We can help you here. It's already been removed. Another potential place is on the A-post at the front of the vehicle but that's been butchered."

"Professional job, then," said Dave Rawson. "Somebody obviously knows his onions and is trying his best to make life hard for us."

"Yes," said Gardener, "because he's also managed to obliterate the area on the windscreen where it's recorded."

"But our Ford garage," added Reilly, "said there are secret etchings in the kite marks on the windscreen glass that could give us an exact date of manufacture."

"And once we have it on a ramp," continued Gardener, "there is a section of the chassis leg at the front of the van which has the number stamped on it."

"So if *that's* not there," said DS Colin Sharp, "then our man really knows what he's doing."

"Sounds like it," said Gardener. "However, other things to study will be the paint and colour code; once we have a sample of the paint, we can probably see the metallic content, possibly the combination of primers and clear coats used, which will also give us the year."

"Sometimes even a month of manufacture, as well as the factory," added Reilly.

"Also, stickers, labels, part numbers can all help. We should employ the services of a member from the stolen motor vehicle crime squad."

"They are like wizards specialising in the dark art of identifying bits of cars," said Reilly, glancing at Gates and Longstaff. "A bit like you two with computers."

"Last resort," added Gardener, "download the information from the ECU, the engine control unit. So, no matter how good our criminal thinks he is, I can't imagine he has eradicated every scrap of information from the van."

Gardener turned to Sharp and Rawson. He informed them of everything the fire chief had told him and Reilly about the accelerant used to torch the van.

"That should be interesting," said Rawson. "There's enough petrol stations around there to have a go at."

"That's assuming it was either bought around here, or the van is local," added Sharp.

"We can but try, Colin," said Gardener. "If we can identify it, then the next step will be to cover all your ANPR/CCTV camera work, which will give us an idea of where the van has been recently."

Gardener glanced at his watch.

"As eager as I am to get you all started, we still need to cover the most important aspect of this scene – the victim."

Chapter Six

"Are there any photos yet?" asked Rawson.

"No," said Gardener, "but I'm not sure they'll help us. He was pretty badly burned, so facial recognition will be difficult."

"And they're not really the sort of photos you can show the general public," added Reilly.

"Didn't you mention laptops?" asked Longstaff.

"Yes, Julie," said Gardener, "but again, the worry is the fire damage. I'm not sure how badly damaged they are but they were twisted up from the heat."

"You never know," said Gates. "We might be able to do something with them."

Gardener nodded. "For now, we'll have to go down the DNA route. If we're lucky, he might have a record."

"Dental records might give us something to go on," said Rawson. "Be nice if he was local because he must have used a dentist around here somewhere."

"We can also trawl our way through missing persons," said Sharp. "There are always plenty of them."

"Good idea," said Gardener. "If we have Bob and Frank back tomorrow, we can perhaps get them started on that."

"You reckoned our victim was probably dead before the fire was started," said Gates. "Any idea what killed him?"

"No," said Gardener. "There's nothing evident. Fitz is going to do the post-mortem as soon as he can, so that could give us another lead."

"But you don't think the shotgun was involved, sir?" asked Edwards.

"Doesn't appear that way," said Reilly. "But again, Fitz might tell us different."

"Might be quite tricky, this one," said Cragg. "We had something like this once. Fella that was set alight inside a car up on the moors. Turned out he were a registered sex offender."

"Christ," said Rawson. "No shortage of suspects for that one, I should imagine."

"No," said Cragg. "I had to look at who his victims were, see if they might be in the frame for it."

"Were there many?" asked Reilly.

"Quite a few," said Cragg. "In the end it was his partner. She'd found out about his history, and she were worried about the shame of it getting out. So she set him on fire thinking she could make it look like a suicide."

"Result!" said Rawson.

"Not so good for her, though," said Gates.

"I bet it still got out," added Longstaff.

"I once had a strange one..." said Reilly.

"I can believe that with you," said Rawson.

Reilly laughed along with everyone else but continued anyway.

"One that springs to mind is a lad shot in the head twice, inside a locked car in the middle of a forest. It took me ages to work out that an Uzi gun can shoot two rounds so quickly that you can shoot yourself in the head twice before you're actually dead!"

"Bloody hell," said Sharp. "I never knew that."

"Seems like we've all had a shooter or a fire to deal with," said Gardener. "My strangest was a man who'd had his head blown off with a shotgun. It all looked cut and dried until I measured his arm against the barrel of the gun and realised he couldn't reach the trigger on his own!

"It was a good lesson in not releasing a scene – which was in the corner of a field – too soon. I had to harass the lab for ages to give me an analysis on what was on the trigger; turned out to be microscopic traces of moss, which I eventually matched to the end of a stick found near the body. He'd put the barrel in his mouth and then reached the trigger with the stick."

"Hell fire," said Rawson. "We're all learning something today."

"The important lesson here is, we can't rule anything out," said Gardener. "It could be suicide, but it doesn't look like it. He could have been shot, and when we get the details of the gun back that might tell us something."

"It should, unless our suspect is a professional," said Cragg. "Believe it or not, I have a section 2 shotgun licence, which is pretty easy to get. You buy an approved cabinet, secure it within the regulations to a wall, pass a few background checks and you're done. Although you can't have any convictions and you must have a referee who also has a licence.

"Someone came out from Leeds Central to check the cabinet was positioned right and that I didn't want to kill the world. Now I can buy as many shotguns as I like, I do clay pigeon shooting, target shooting etc. Point I'm coming to, every gun has a serial number, it's registered and held on a licence. If I buy one from a dealer or private seller, I have to tell the police within a week who I bought it from, and what the serial number is. The seller also informs the police of whom he sold it to and what the serial number is, and the police will transfer it off their licence and onto mine. They are meant to keep track of every gun in the UK in this way."

"So," said Gardener, "despite it being a tricky one we have plenty to go on. I realize it's Saturday and we may not collect much either today or tomorrow, but we'll give it a go anyway. You guys have your actions, Sean and I need to visit the scrapyard on East Ings Lane and speak to the people who run it, see if *they* know anything."

Chapter Seven

It was late afternoon before Gardener and Reilly pulled into DM Metals at the end of East Ings Lane. It was an old-style scrapyard that very probably contravened health and safety laws. Most of the cars were piled three high, around the perimeter. The ones in the middle of the yard were scattered – two high – which pretty much formed a maze, but with gaps that Gardener could see through.

To his right was a large portacabin. At the very back of the yard he noticed a tatty caravan. Surprisingly, there were no guard dogs, but he *was* pleased to see CCTV cameras.

"Morning."

Gardener turned to see a man stepping from the portacabin. He was well built – very stocky, with a head of thinning brown hair. As he came nearer, Gardener noticed his blue eyes. The voice was smooth with a deep Yorkshire accent. He had a well-trimmed beard with a narrow moustache. He was on a mobile but waved them forward into the cabin.

Inside, on the left was an office behind a counter, with a desk containing computer equipment. On the wall were a couple of corkboards filled with sheets of paper that had been scribbled on. The section on the right contained a small kitchen, housing a table with a newspaper on, four chairs, a sink, cupboards, and tea and coffee making facilities. A door at the far end probably led to a toilet. A radio tuned to a local station stood on the draining board.

The man pointed to a seat and then gestured drinks with his hand and held up two fingers to perhaps suggest that's how long he would be. He continued with his conversation, grabbing a pen and some paper.

"I can have him down to you first thing in the morning," he said. "We have a flatbed and trailer big enough for those two vehicles."

The man wrote down technical details, such as directions and postcode. He finished his meeting before placing the phone on the counter. He slipped through to the kitchen area.

"Sorry about that, always something." He held out a hand and said, "Derrick Mitchell."

He was dressed in a boilersuit, and Gardener noticed he was wearing a gold watch and necklace with a locket.

The SIO introduced himself and Reilly and asked if they could ask him some questions about the events surrounding the van fire they had discovered earlier.

"I've heard about it," said Mitchell. "Kettle's just boiled and I'm parched. You fellas want a brew?"

"Go on, then," said Reilly.

With the tea made, Mitchell took a seat and asked how he could help.

"Business good?" asked Reilly.

"Mad," said Mitchell. "Always something to do."

"I imagine you *were* here yesterday," said Gardener. "We're just combing the area to see what – if anything – people saw."

"I'm here every day," said Mitchell, "but I can't say I saw anything. I were here till eight o'clock last night, though."

Mitchell stood up and grabbed his phone and returned to the table.

"If you have a look here" – he turned the phone round so they could see it – "I sent my last email at seven forty-five. Once I'd cleared up, I left. About eight."

"You didn't notice any unusual activity, no large vans kicking about?" asked Reilly.

"No," said Mitchell. "But I've got CCTV if you want to look through it. Not sure how much it will show you because it's not very good, temperamental to say the least."

Mitchell took them to the computer and checked what was recorded. He was seen leaving at eight as he'd mentioned. They then fast-forwarded the footage until virtually half an hour before Gardener and Reilly arrived. The problem was, the cameras were really only focused on the gates and not any distance down the lane.

Back at the table, Mitchell asked, "Was it just a fire, or a bit more serious?"

"We found someone in it," said Reilly.

"Oh, Christ, that's nasty. I take it he or she is dead?"

"I'm afraid so."

Mitchell took a sip of tea. "I wish I could help you more, but I can't. We're a bit out of the way here. As you can see, it's a dead end. Only people that come round here are those who want to scrap a car or buy parts."

"How long have you been here, Mr Mitchell?" asked Gardener.

"Bloody hell, now you're asking. Years. I started here when I left school, with an old character called Fred Carnaby. He was running it then. To start with, all I did were make tea, and strip vehicles for parts. Then I passed my test and old Fred had me collecting cars to scrap and crush from all over the country. I loved it, did it for five years. I only decided to stay yard bound when old Fred said he were giving it another year before retiring. I learned as much as I could, but what I really needed were the money to buy Fred out. Our Terry, my brother, came to my rescue."

"Is Terry still around?" asked Reilly.

"I'm afraid not," said Mitchell, lowering his head.

Gardener suspected some personal tragedy, so he moved on.

"Is it fair to say that you would know everyone round here, Mr Mitchell?"

"Just about. Can't say there's anyone I know who'd do summat like that, though. I've not really heard anything either, but to be honest I work long hours and keep myself to myself. Bit boring, really."

"Talking of knowing everyone," said Reilly. "We gather you employ someone called Frankie."

Mitchell rolled his eyes. "You've met him, then. What's he been up to now?"

"Nothing that we know of, Mr Mitchell," said Gardener. "But he told us that he lived *and* worked here." The SIO glanced around. "I can't see him living in here, and I can't see anything out there in the yard, so is what he told us true?"

"Oh, aye," said Mitchell, standing up. "Follow me."

Mitchell stepped out of the portacabin and stared down the yard, pointing to the caravan that Gardener had seen on arrival, which appeared to have survived a nuclear attack. He was sure the colour had once been white, now it was green with mould – and black with dirt. Every panel appeared to have a dent in it, and even though it was a bit of a distance away, it was impossible to see through any of the windows. The bird shit actually helped its appearance.

"That's where he lives," said Mitchell.

"He lives in there?" asked Reilly.

"Oh aye," said Mitchell. "It's a real step up from what he used to have."

"Which was?"

"A makeshift wooden shelter in the same place, held together with nuts and bolts, with a piece of tarpaulin over the top."

"What happened to that?" asked Gardener.

"Blew apart one night in a bad storm. Next morning, I picked the caravan up when I went to collect a number of vehicles from one of the local garages. I took it away as a favour, intending to scrap it, but Frankie begged me not to."

"Look at the state of it," said Reilly. "What's the inside like?"

"I'm not *that* stupid." Mitchell laughed. "Look around you, what do you see?"

"A scrapyard."

"Precisely, a mess," replied Mitchell. "But I'll lay odds it's cleaner and safer out here than being in there, especially with his breath."

Gardener couldn't argue with that one. "What do you know about him?"

"To be honest, not much. Don't know his friends, or if he has any family, or where he actually comes from."

"How come he has a job with you?"

"He's cheap, and he's reliable. Apart from that, somebody has to give him a job and this is about the only place he could work. We rub along okay. I don't mind helping."

At that point, the door opened and Frankie squeezed himself through the gap, instantly disappearing downwards. A cloud of dust rose up. Despite his bulk he was back on his feet quickly.

Mitchell shouted loud enough to wake the dead and waved him over. Frankie appeared none too keen, glancing right and left and then upwards. Finally, he sheepishly made a move. For any normal person it should have taken half a minute, but Frankie took longer because he kept stepping out of view.

"Where does he keep disappearing to?" asked Reilly.

"He's checking his money," said Mitchell.

"Money?" questioned Gardener.

Mitchell laughed and nodded. "He thinks I don't know about it. He's got tins scattered all over the yard, all full of money. You see that old Minor 1000 over there, stacked up on bricks?"

Gardener nodded.

"The biggest stash is in there. Thousands. He honestly believes I don't know that he has it. Me! It's my bloody scrapyard."

"How *does* he have it?" asked Reilly.

"He's got all sorts of little scams and sidelines going on," said Mitchell. "Nothing illegal, but he sells all sorts of stuff from the yard. I just ignore it. He's not really doing any harm. I don't pay him a lot, and he has the use of the caravan, but by far and away the biggest amounts come from the nags."

"The horses?" questioned Reilly.

"Yes," replied Mitchell, "the horses. He's been banned from just about every betting shop in the area. We don't know whether he just has the luck of the devil, or inside information, but he wins stupid amounts, and the bookies have no way of stopping him. Like I say, he's not doing anything illegal."

Frankie finally appeared in front of them as if by magic.

"Get yourself in the cabin," Mitchell said. "These two gentlemen want a word with you."

"Me?" said Frankie.

Here we go again, thought Gardener.

* * *

Thirty minutes of questions, mostly from Frankie, revealed he had seen and heard nothing. He was a human safe; any information he had stayed on the inside. He barely spoke at all, only to ask his own questions, and avoided answering them wherever possible. His eyes were all over the place but despite all that he didn't appear uncomfortable. Gardener didn't know if he was stupid, evasive, or simply a genius in disguise.

CCTV confirmed he had been in his caravan from around five o'clock onwards and had not left. He claimed he neither heard nor saw the fire. The CCTV cameras did pick up Frankie leaving his caravan shortly before Gardener and Reilly arrived at the crime scene.

Reilly made some comment about Frankie being the next prime minister because he had the major quality – he never answered a question directly, and actually didn't make any sense when he did.

Gardener turned his attention back to the owner of the yard.

"What time did you arrive today, Mr Mitchell?"

"Quite late for me," he replied. "Around dinner time."

Frankie nodded his head so severely that Gardener thought it might fall off.

"I had some business in Bursley Bridge and Bramfield," Mitchell said, "and also made a trip to the bank, so it was around one o'clock when I got here. I drove past the chaos in the field. One of your chaps stopped me and asked a few questions."

"Okay," said Gardener, knowing he could check that. "I think we're about done for now. If we need anything else we can find you here. Where do you live, Mr Mitchell?"

"An old chapel on Main Street in Morton, just north of Bursley Bridge. You can't miss it. It's on the A170, opposite the Spar shop and post office. I bought the building twelve years ago in an auction."

"Sounds nice," said Gardener.

"We'll be away and leave you in peace now, guys, thank you for your time," said Reilly.

"What's the rush?" asked Gardener.

"Kempton 3.15, I need to get this bet on."

Frankie's eyes lit up like a UFO. "Which one?"

"Pardon," said Reilly.

"Which one?" asked Frankie, almost frothing at the mouth.

Gardener glanced at Mitchell. He was smiling.

"Do you know a bit about the nags, then, Frankie?" asked Reilly.

Frankie simply shrugged his shoulders. Reilly opened the paper and studied the form, before sliding it across the table.

"I have a wee fancy for that one myself, Irish Rover. Good price at eight to one. I think I'll stick a tenner on. And I can tell you, Frankie, I'm a good judge of horses, so I am."

Frankie didn't touch the paper. Instead he made a massive show of trying to find his glasses, and then admitted that he couldn't and asked Reilly to read them out, along with their form.

After he'd finished, Frankie said, "Irish Rover, you say?"

"Aye," said Reilly. "A definite winner if ever I saw one."

"Not this time."

"Sorry?" said Reilly.

"You want Alford Star."

Reilly checked the starting price. "It's thirty-three to one."

"Stick thirty quid on it," said Frankie.

Chapter Eight

After the police had left and Mitchell had seen them off, he slipped back into the cabin.

"Right, Frankie, I have a job for you."

Frankie didn't actually reply. He was staring at the paper that Reilly had left. Mitchell was never quite sure if he could read because of the rigmarole they went through every time he sent him somewhere. Mitchell always had to set the satnav for Frankie, and he had to print a picture of wherever he was going and give that to him as well.

"I need you to collect a couple of cars from a dealer at Scotch Corner."

Frankie stood up and simply nodded. He took everything from Mitchell and then said he was going back to his caravan for something to eat.

Mitchell didn't even like to think what that would be. Frankie was a human garbage disposal. If you had any food left over from your meal or your pack up, Frankie's favourite line was 'waste not, want not' and he would finish it for you. He wasn't fussy. Mitchell had actually once seen him mixing a whole range of different foods over his plate: bacon, mash, peas, beans and God knew what else – it made no difference to him, it was all food. He went to the local supermarket at closing time, which served two purposes: if he *did* have to pay for anything it was bound to be cheap. Alternatively, there was always plenty in the skip – still packaged.

Once Frankie had left, Mitchell sat down at the table, wondering what was wrong with his employee. He knew very well you couldn't drag an answer out of Frankie if he didn't want to tell you anything – even if you sat and questioned him for days or threatened to torture him to death. But Mitchell knew him well enough to know that something was distracting him.

But what?

He thought about the van fire, and the body inside, and then Frankie's odd mood. Were they connected?

Mitchell would have to bide his time. It would all come out in the wash, especially if Frankie had a drink.

Chapter Nine

Sunday lunchtime saw Gardener and Reilly in the incident room. Twenty-four hours had passed since the crime had been reported, a time period crucial to any investigation. Gardener realized they still had very little to go on, which is why he'd asked the team to stop by and give him an update – anything at all that would be useful.

Edwards and Benson were already in the room. Gates and Longstaff appeared with coffees in their hands. Sharp and Rawson were still out.

Gardener had a bottle of water with him. Reilly was sitting with his arms over the back of the chair, with rather a large grin on his face.

"What's put you in a happy mood?" asked Gardener.

"A horse called Alford Star."

"It didn't?"

"Bloody well did. Old Frankie boy knows his horses, I'll give him that."

"Did you put thirty on?"

"I did. Romped home at thirty-three to one and collected myself just over a grand."

"I think we'll have to pay Frankie another visit," said Gardener.

"All in the line of duty, of course."

"Of course. Sandwiches on you, then?"

Gardener turned to address the team. "I realize there may not be a lot to report, so while we're waiting for Colin and Dave I'll update you with what we've just learned. During the last half hour, Head of Scenes of Crime, Steve

Fenton dropped by with the gun found in the back of the van, and the two laptops."

"How are the laptops looking?" asked Gates.

"Wasted," said Reilly.

He left the chair, crossed the room to a table, grabbed an evidence bag and passed it to the women.

"I see what you mean," said Longstaff.

Both devices were melted and twisted, and Gardener couldn't possibly see how any information could have survived.

"We can have a go," said Gates. "It doesn't look good, but you never really know. There could be something worth salvaging."

"Might be helpful," said Gardener.

"What about the gun, sir?" asked Paul Benson.

Reilly produced another evidence bag.

"It fared slightly better," said Gardener. "As you'd expect, it's fire-damaged and the serial number has been ground off. Criminals do that so we can't trace it back to anywhere."

"The barrel's been sawn off as well," said Reilly, "so someone had a serious use for it. But sawing off a shotgun isn't as simple as it sounds. People tend to try and make them as short as possible so they're easy to hide. Cut down the stock to just after the pistol grip, which is a bad idea."

Reilly pointed to the gun to illustrate what he was saying.

"The recoil is impossible to handle and the shot coming out can be so haphazard it can blow back to take your hand off or even blind you. Add a couple of inches after the fore and it'll be much better. We know this is a 20-bore, which is smaller and lighter than a 12-bore, but just as deadly."

"There is a possibility, that even without the serial number," said Gardener, "we might be able to do something with it. We have had it dusted for prints."

"I can't see how," said Edwards. "Surely without the serial number we'll be snookered."

"Maybe," said Gardener. "But we have the oracle on our side, he might know something."

"Where is Maurice?" asked Benson.

"He was on his way in here when he took a phone call," said Gardener.

Turning his attention to Gates and Longstaff, he asked if they had discovered anything at all about the van.

Gates informed him it was now with Stoneacre Ford in York. They'd persuaded the site manager, Scott Anderson, to open the body shop for them so they could make a quick inspection.

"The main thing to report," said Gates, "is that the chassis leg section that contains the chassis number has been removed. The site manager pointed out where it should be."

"But at least we have paint samples to pass on," said Longstaff.

"We have spoken to the stolen motor vehicle crime squad. They have the samples."

"Scott Anderson actually contacted Ford for us, and they are going to set up a meeting at the garage to download the ECU to see what they can come up with."

"It's still on the van, then?" said Reilly.

"Yes," said Gates, "and it's not fire-damaged."

"That's something," said Gardener. "Any idea when?"

"They know time is of the essence so they said they will give it their best attention."

"Whoever is responsible," said Benson, "they seem pretty professional, removing everything they can think of."

"Could be an outside gang," said Reilly.

"But it's a small community," said Gates. "Surely an outsider would have been noticed."

"I'm inclined to agree," said Gardener. "But the area is very barren, even Bob North said they didn't usually see anyone they didn't know."

"We should speak to Maurice," said Reilly. "He might be able to enlighten us if something else has been going on in the area."

"I'll have a word with him after the meeting," said Gardener. "Anything on house-to-house?"

"Nothing, yet, sir," said Edwards. "As you just said, it's barren, not many houses, and those we have spoken to were in bed at the likely time this would have happened."

Gardener nodded. He really couldn't expect too much. He was about to speak again when Sharp and Rawson walked through the door.

"Just in time," said Gardener.

"Maybe," said Sharp. "But we don't have much at the moment."

"We met up with Roy Dodgson this morning," said Rawson. "He's the sniffer expert."

"Oh, good, did we find anything?"

"He was telling us that the most commonly used accelerants are petrol, kerosene, mineral turps, and diesel, which are generally complex mixtures of hydrocarbon molecules," said Rawson. "He also told us a lot of boring shit about these hydrocarbons having similar chemical properties. Went on for ages about it and told us exactly what the sniffer did."

"Most of which we've forgotten," said Sharp.

"The upshot was," said Rawson, "he collected samples from the area where the van was and said he'll be back to us tomorrow with some news."

"Okay," said Gardener. "It could be worse."

With that, Cragg entered the room with two sheets of paper in his hand.

"I have something very interesting here regarding that phone call I had to take. Well, two phone calls to be precise."

"Go on, Maurice," said Gardener.

"Both calls concerned a MISPER. It's a very strange affair; two different women have both reported the same man as missing."

"Who's the man?" asked Gardener.

"His name's Davey Challenger – lives and works locally."

"Who are the two people reporting it?" asked Gardener.

"One's his wife, Grace Challenger."

"And the other?" asked Reilly.

"His girlfriend," said Cragg. "A lady called Monica Rushby. So I'm just wondering if we have a connection to our van fire."

Chapter Ten

After taking all the details from Cragg, Gardener and Reilly pulled up outside Grace Challenger's house, a two-bedroom bungalow on the left side of Whitby Road in Bursley Bridge, opposite a new housing development. Reilly parked the car. Gardener immediately noticed a hugely colourful garden. To the left of the house was a double garage.

"Nice place," said Reilly.

"Someone's certainly put a lot of effort into *making* it nice," said Gardener. "Bet my dad would love to see this."

As they exited the car and walked down the drive, the lady of the house met them at the front door.

Gardener was quite taken aback. She was tall, approaching six feet, very slim, with long auburn hair in a wavy cut, dropping onto her shoulders in loose waves, emphasizing the cheekbones and elongating the face. Her make-up was completely flawless.

"Ooh." She put her hand to her mouth. "You startled me."

She was dressed casually, in jeans and a Barbour jacket but even they were the latest fashion. She was wearing gardening gloves.

"Grace Challenger?" asked Gardener.

"Yes?"

He introduced himself and Reilly, displaying his warrant card.

"You must excuse me," said Grace, glancing down at her clothes. "I've been in the garden. I find it very therapeutic."

"You and my dad both," said Gardener.

"Have you come about my missing husband?" asked Grace. She stepped back from the door, further into the porch. "Please, come in."

As both officers did, Grace pointed to a shoe rack and asked if they'd mind removing their shoes.

Once through the door, Gardener could see why. The house was immaculate. A long hall with living and dining rooms on either side led through to a kitchen at the back. Two further rooms led to two en-suite bedrooms, and he also noticed another separate bathroom, because all the doors were open.

Grace led them into the living room decorated with a cream carpet with a pile so thick Gardener immediately thought he'd shrunk. Oils adorned the pale lemon walls, mainly of wildlife and countryside scenes. The suite was a dark brown, leather Chesterfield. A log burner nestled into a brick-built fireplace, above which was a mirror. A six-sided swivel table took centre stage in the room with a silver candlestick holder polished to perfection – a little like Grace.

"Can I make either of you some tea?"

"Tea would be nice," said Gardener.

"Please take a seat, I'll be back shortly."

"This is some place," said Reilly.

"Isn't it just," replied Gardener. "I'd like to know what everyone does for a living."

Grace returned five minutes later with everything they needed on a tea tray. Before sitting down, she poured a drink for everyone and set out a plate of mixed biscuits. Gardener smiled. Food always went down well with his partner; made him warmer, more responsive.

"Have you found him?" Grace asked.

"Not yet, Mrs Challenger," replied Gardener. "We would like to ask you a few questions if we may?"

"Of course."

"How old is he?" asked Reilly.

"Fifty-one."

"Can you describe him?" asked Gardener. "Or do you have a photograph we could borrow, please?"

"One moment," said Grace, leaving the table.

Gardener noticed that everything she did was almost angelic – every movement suited her name. He doubted she was the kind of woman who flapped easily; she would be well able to hold her own in any kind of company.

Grace returned with a photo album, leafing through until she found what she wanted, before removing one and passing it to Gardener. The man in the photo was tall, like Grace, with grey hair, blue eyes and well-maintained teeth. He had a ruddy complexion, the kind usually acquired through working outdoors. Gardener noticed an expensive watch on his wrist, and a gold chain around his neck.

"What does he do for a living, Mrs Challenger?" asked Gardener.

"He is a parcel delivery driver for the post office. He had been a postman but took the offer of the driving job. He much preferred that, as he likes being outside. He refused an office job on more than one occasion."

Gardener struggled to see how a delivery driver for the post office could maintain the house they were in, but then, he didn't know the whole story.

"Do you work?" he asked.

"No," replied Grace. "But I've been quite lucky because an aunt left me a considerable amount when she passed away, and I'm careful."

"Does your husband have any hobbies?" asked Reilly.

"Probably the local pub," said Grace, before quickly adding, "oh, dear, that sounds awful, doesn't it?"

"Truthful, maybe," said Reilly.

"I don't mean that he is an alcoholic. Davey often goes for a quick drink, but rarely stays out late due to the hours he sometimes works. He's a member of the darts team."

"Which pub?" Gardener asked.

"The Rose Inn on Bridge Street," replied Grace.

Gardener was busy mentally working his way through possible associates: neighbours, friends and members of the darts team were high on his list.

"Is he at the pub every night or just on darts nights?" asked Reilly.

"He goes maybe two or three times a week."

"Do you join him?"

"No, I'm afraid not, officer," said Grace. "Pubs are not really my scene."

Gardener suspected as much, wondering how close Grace and her husband were.

"Can you tell us about the last time you saw him?" asked the SIO.

"That would be Friday night. He left here around seven-thirty. He said he had a darts match. He was team captain."

"And where were you?"

"I was here all night," said Grace.

"How did he seem?" asked Reilly.

"Do I have to be honest?" asked Grace.

Reilly had been about to take a drink but stopped. "We'd appreciate it."

Gardener wondered what she meant by the comment.

"Is there something you need to tell us, Mrs Challenger?"

"It's nothing bad," said Grace. "I suppose every marriage has its ups and downs. I'm probably not the easiest of women to get along with but it's because I care. He works hard and I like things to be right."

"I appreciate that, Mrs Challenger," said Gardener. "Going back to the night you last saw him, do you have the feeling something was bothering him?"

"Sorry," replied Grace, "I do have a tendency to waffle on. You must stop me if I am. Anyway, he seemed okay, but we haven't spoken a lot of late. I feel that he's been very secretive. He spends a lot more time out of the house than usual."

"Do you have any idea where he is on those occasions?" asked Gardener, well aware that two people had reported him missing, one of which was a girlfriend.

"I'm afraid I don't."

"He never told you where he was going?" asked Reilly.

"Not very often, unless it was darts, but I don't think they played more than once a week."

"Did you ever check?"

"Ooh no, officer. I felt sure that if something was wrong, he would tell me. You have to have trust in a marriage, or you don't have anything."

Gardener nodded. "Today is Sunday, and you last saw him on Friday, and you've had no contact since?"

"No."

"Have you tried his mobile?" asked Reilly.

"A few times," replied Grace. "They all go to voicemail."

Gardener figured that wherever the phone was it must be switched off, which meant they were unlikely to track him through that. The best they might be able to do if they found it would be triangulate the signal from the nearest three masts up to the point it was switched off.

"Have you spoken to everyone you can think of, Mrs Challenger? Colleagues, work mates, neighbours; anyone who might have seen him, or whom he might be staying with?"

"Those that I can remember," she replied. "The neighbours don't really know anything. His workmates haven't seen him, nor any of his friends."

"It isn't normal for him to leave for long absences without contacting you, then?" asked Gardener.

"No. He usually told me where he was, until recently, like I said earlier. I don't know what the hell he could have been up to but I'm getting worried now. This isn't natural."

"I'm sure there's a reasonable explanation," said Reilly.

"I hope so," said Grace.

Gardener asked if he could have a list of contacts before they left, with phone numbers and addresses if possible, as well as her husband's number. He also figured it was cards on the table time. He almost felt like he was deceiving her. He confirmed what they had discovered yesterday, and whilst they had no reason to think the victim in the van was her husband, he explained that the investigation was still ongoing, and they had to explore every avenue. There was a faint possibility she may have to prepare herself for a shock.

Grace suddenly blanched. "Oh my God. Is it my husband? Is he dead? What the hell was he doing in a burnt-out van in the middle of a field?"

"Mrs Challenger," said Gardener. "We really don't know who is in the van, and I hope it *isn't* your husband, but I do need you to be aware of what we found, because I wouldn't like you to hear anything from anyone else, or read something in the newspaper that you feel we should have told you."

"So it might not be him?"

"We have no evidence to suspect it is at the moment."

"Does the person in the van look like him?" asked Grace, pointing at the photo.

Gardener glanced at it. "I'm afraid we can't tell."

He made a mental note to ask Fitz if any jewellery was found on the body, because he couldn't remember seeing any.

Grace put her hands to her mouth. "Oh my God, is it that bad?"

Gardener didn't say anything.

"Can I see him?" she asked.

"Not yet, Mrs Challenger," said Gardener. "At least not until we are a little further into the investigation, and not unless we are sure it is your husband."

"Just to ask again, Grace, love," said Reilly, "you have no idea where his phone is?"

"Not at all."

"Does he have any computer equipment?"

"Yes, he has a laptop and an iPad, which he uses mostly for work."

"Does he keep them in the house?"

"Not really. The iPad is always in his van, sometimes he brings the laptop in to browse the Internet and buy things from Amazon."

She glanced over to a coffee table at the side of one of the armchairs.

"If it was in the house, that's where it would be."

It wasn't.

Gardener let the dust settle before asking if Grace was okay. She nodded.

"Is there someone you'd like us to call, Mrs Challenger, to come and sit with you?"

"Not that I can think of. We have no children. My parents only live in York, and my sister, Fiona, lives in Thirsk. I can call them if I need them, but sometimes I think it's better to be on your own. People don't know what to say to you. And in this instance, we don't know anything either. Like you said, it may not be him."

"Does your husband have any family?"

"I'm afraid not. His parents died a few years ago and he is an only child."

"You seem very well organized," said Gardener. "If there *is* anything you need, you must please ask us."

Grace nodded.

"I would like to ask one question if I may?" said Gardener. "I appreciate the photo, but I wondered if you had a comb, or a hairbrush, or maybe even a toothbrush that we could take."

"Why do you need those?" asked Grace.

"So we can compare the DNA of your husband to the man in the van, which would help to confirm or exclude who it is."

Grace said she understood and left the room. She returned very quickly with all three in a plastic bag, and a printout on A4 sheets of contacts.

Chapter Eleven

The pair of them stepped into Grace's porch to retrieve their footwear. Once outside in the warm, dry weather they strolled down the path at the side of the house. A large section of flowers in every colour known to man decorated the area.

"You keep a lovely garden, Grace, love," said Reilly.

"Thank you."

"It must keep you busy," said Gardener.

"You can say that again, but it's so rewarding."

Gardener perused the mass of different colours, and it was only then that he noticed it appeared to be divided into sections with almost military precision: herbs, flowers, fruit, veg, and shrubs. He wouldn't have minded betting that everything else in her life was the same.

"You obviously know what you're doing," said Gardener. "You grow a lot of fruit and vegetables?"

"Oh, yes," said Grace, still slightly distracted. "I believe in healthy eating and you can't get any healthier than produce from your own garden. There's nothing better than collecting it all in a basket and preparing your meals, a bit like that chef on the TV, Nigel Slater. He grows everything he needs in his garden. I love watching his programs. I have all of his books."

"Bet it saves you a fortune at the shops," said Reilly.

"It does. Of course, you have to be careful what you choose to grow. There are certain varieties you should steer clear of."

"Isn't that only with wild mushrooms?" asked Reilly.

"Definitely those."

"That's me out, then, I wouldn't know one from another."

"Stick to the supermarket, then, officer, much safer."

"Do you have mushrooms here?"

"No," replied Grace. "Too much trouble to grow, and believe it or not, I am actually allergic to them, but I have almost everything else."

"Thank you," said Gardener, "I'm sure we've taken enough of your time, Mrs Challenger. We appreciate your cooperation. I will be in touch when I know something."

"Thank you," said Grace, staring at the ground.

They left the house and once they were in the car, Reilly asked, "What do you think?"

"I'm not sure. It's easy to feel sorry for her," said Gardener. "She's very naive, almost childlike. I think everything in her life is in order, with a well-maintained routine, and I think we've just driven a truck through it. I almost felt like she was in denial; that it might be her husband in the van, but until we say it is, she will go on believing that he'll come home at any moment. Having said that, we don't know either."

Reilly started the car. "I know what you mean, and I hope for her sake he does. For now, let's go and see what the other woman in his life has to say."

Chapter Twelve

Half an hour later, Reilly drove the car though the centre of Bramfield. Gardener noticed Armitage's hardware store was still there, and he wondered if the old man had made good on his promise of selling the place and retiring, following a horrific killing spree involving his nephew.

Within a few minutes they pulled up outside a small bungalow on the corner of Orchard Road. The garden was neat but nothing like the one they had seen at Grace Challenger's place. He noticed a small conservatory, a car porch but no car, and a garage.

They left their vehicle and approached the front door, then knocked and waited. A buxom blonde dressed in a cream skirt and top answered quite quickly. She was neither thin nor fat, but nestled somewhere in between, with a chest large enough to divert a man's attention. Her blonde hair was fashioned in the style of a bob, finishing on her shoulders. She had brown eyes, a chubby nose and clean, white teeth.

"Can I help you?" she asked.

Gardener tipped his hat and they introduced themselves. He explained the reason for the visit was an investigation into a missing persons case, and he wondered if they might ask her a few questions relating to it. She stood to one side to allow them in, before leading them into a kitchen. The house was tidy but lived-in. A couple of magazines littered the kitchen worktop. A few items of shopping, mainly tins and packets were next to them, suggesting she may already have been out and not been back long. A radio on the window ledge was set to a low volume. The music appeared vintage, which was confirmed when the jingle announced they were listening to Gold UK.

She asked them to sit at the table and if they would like tea. They declined as they'd recently had some.

"I've just brewed. You don't mind if I have one, do you? It's just that I need to take my medication."

"Not at all," said Gardener. "Is it anything serious?"

"Depends on how you look at it; Addison's disease."

"Can't say I've heard of that one, Monica, love," said Reilly.

"I'm not surprised, it is pretty rare. The problem is with the glands near my kidneys. It means my body doesn't produce enough cortisol, or aldosterone."

"What sort of symptoms do you get?" asked Reilly.

"Bloody awful," said Monica. "Fatigue, muscle weakness, low moods and loss of appetite, which leads to weight loss, increased thirst."

"How long have you had it?" asked Reilly.

"It came on after Covid. Everyone thought it was long Covid, but it isn't. Don't know whether I'm pleased or not."

Gardener nodded. "What do you do for a living, Miss Rushby?"

She took a drink and her medication and then addressed the question.

"I'm a maternity nurse at the Bramfield Community Hospital, but I've worked in all of the departments over the years."

That explained the medical knowledge, thought Gardener. "Is it a big hospital?"

"It's an inpatient and outpatient unit, provides care for patients over eighteen, mostly minor injuries."

"I reckon you've been quite busy over the last couple of years," said Reilly.

"You could say that."

Gardener appreciated her no-nonsense attitude. Her answers appeared to be straight. She was a completely different animal to Grace Challenger. Given what they had heard of the affair, he wondered how much the three people involved actually knew collectively.

He decided to tackle the reason they were there and asked about the man she had reported missing.

"Davey is lovely, really. Talkative and well mannered. Good with his hands." When she'd said that, she covered her mouth with her hands. "Sorry, I didn't mean it that way. I meant he is good at fixing things. My mother always says my mouth gets me into trouble."

"Where did you meet?" asked Reilly.

"My friend Trudi, from the hospital, asked me if I'd like a weekend away. It was a jewellery convention. Her husband was away on business all weekend and she thought it would be nice to get away. The shifts I work, you never get the chance to go out so I thought it would make a nice change. That was six months ago. Never thought I'd meet the love of my life."

Gardener found the phrase an interesting one. Monica clearly saw it as a serious relationship. He wondered how Davey Challenger saw it, but at least it hadn't been a one-night stand, so he must have felt something.

Gardener then noticed that Monica Rushby was wearing a necklace and a matching bracelet that he'd never seen the like of before; it was quite unique.

Reilly had obviously twigged, and he asked her about it.

"I make jewellery," said Monica, "as a way of relieving the stress of the job, which can sometimes happen.

Everything I make is different, and I sell the pieces on to friends to cover expenses. Any profit I make, I give to a local charity supported by the hospital for the baby unit." She stared at her own bracelet. "I'm quite proud of them, something you'll never see in the shops."

"Where does your boyfriend work?" asked Reilly, returning to the subject at hand.

"I'm not really sure."

"You're not sure?"

"Well, he says it's quite a high-ranking position and the company is government-owned and that he travels quite a lot, but he hasn't actually told me where he goes or what he does. I thought it might be the secret service or something."

Gardener found that interesting as well. But he supposed a parcel delivery driver could be all of those things he had claimed.

"Can you let me have his address?" asked Gardener.

"He lives in a small village about half an hour's drive away, called Morton, somewhere on the main street."

Gardener took down the details, wondering what the hell was going on. He wondered if they *were* in fact talking about a different man who happened to have the same name.

"What about his friends?" asked Reilly. "Have you met any of them?"

Monica's expression changed to one of slight shock.

"To be honest, I haven't. We spend a lot of time here; we like each other's company, have many of the same interests and I love to cook, and he likes eating, so we never go out much."

Gardener figured that would suit Challenger; at least he wouldn't be seen and recognized.

"Do you spend any time at *his* house?"

Monica's brow furrowed. "Now you come to mention it, I don't think we've ever been to his house other than the time we had a weekend away and he had to quickly stop and rush in for something."

"Did you go in with him?"

"No, I waited in the car."

Gardener pondered over that one. What could he have possibly been doing?

"Don't you find it unusual that you've been in a relationship with someone for six months and you're not quite sure where he works, who his friends are, and have never been to his house?" asked Reilly.

"When you put it like that," said Monica, "it does sound strange, but to be perfectly honest, it doesn't matter too much to me. He makes me feel special, exclusive, like I am the only thing in his life. And believe me, officer, I've been messed about by quite a few men in my time."

"When was the last time you saw him?" asked Reilly.

"It would have been last Tuesday night. We did speak on the phone on Thursday night. He said he'd been really busy and that he might not see me for a week or so. He never explained why but he seemed in really good spirits. We talked about a move to the Algarve–"

"Portugal?" asked Gardener.

"Yes. He's been talking about it for a while, says he is ready to sell up and move abroad. On the Tuesday night he even brought round some brochures showing properties we could rent whilst we search for a home."

"You're planning to go as well?" asked Gardener.

Monica finished her tea. "It's a big move, I know, but there's nothing to keep me here. I'm not married, and I have no kids."

"Any family?" asked Gardener.

She nodded. "I have, but most of them have moved away. My mother's the only one here; she lives in Bursley Bridge. One of my sisters, Sylvia, lives in Canada Water in London; the other, Olivia, emigrated to New Zealand with the love of her life about ten years ago."

Gardener decided to move on.

"And you've not heard anything from him since Thursday night, or seen him since Tuesday?"

"No." She folded her arms and Gardener noticed a worried expression cross her features. "I know I don't see him all the time because we are both so busy, but I thought I would have seen or heard something by now. You don't think anything's happened to him, do you?"

Gardener mentioned the reason they had come was not simply her missing boyfriend. He felt it only right to mention the van fire.

Monica suddenly stood up and put her hands to her mouth once again. "Oh no, you don't think it's him, do you?"

"At the moment, Miss Rushby, we don't know who it is," replied Gardener. "Do you have a photo of him?"

"Yes," she said, leaving the kitchen and slipping into the living room.

She returned with one in a frame, which confirmed they were talking about the same man Grace Challenger was married to.

Monica sat down, crossing and uncrossing her hands.

"Oh, God, I hope he's okay. The man in the van isn't my Davey, is it?"

Gardener passed the photo to his partner.

"It's too early to say." As a way of distracting her he asked, "Can I ask where you were on Friday night, Miss Rushby?"

"Working at the hospital, pulling an all-nighter. We're still a bit short-staffed with this Covid lark. I'll be pleased when we can all get back to normal, I don't mind telling you."

You and me both, thought Gardener.

"Have you tried calling his mobile since?"

"Yes, three times. It always goes to voicemail."

Gardener realized with what little Monica Rushby actually knew about her boyfriend, there was no one else she could call.

"Does he have any personal items here like a toothbrush, or a comb, a hairbrush maybe?" he asked.

"Yes," she said, leaving the kitchen once again. She returned with all three in a bag. "I suppose that's for DNA, isn't it?"

"It might help to identify who is in the van, Miss Rushby," said Gardener.

Figuring there wasn't much else he could ask her he decided to call it a day. She saw them out and he said he would be in touch as soon as he knew something.

"Interesting," said Gardener in the car.

"She's a different animal to Grace Challenger," said Reilly.

"So is Grace's husband if what she said is anything to go by. What the hell is going on?"

"We obviously have a man who likes leading a double life," said Reilly. "What a can of worms this could be. If our man in the van is Davey Challenger, has he upset someone bad enough to end up dead?"

"And if he has," said Gardener, "who is it, and how did he upset them?"

Gardener's phone rang. When he'd finished the conversation, he turned to Reilly.

"Fitz would like to speak to us."

Chapter Thirteen

Gardener and Reilly were sitting opposite Fitz in his office. All three men had a cup of Irish Cream flavoured coffee. Reilly had an empty Kit Kat wrapper in front of him, and he was now opening a Double Decker bar. Some kind of light opera music that Gardener neither knew nor cared about was on in the background.

"I dread to think what they're going to find when they finally have to open *you* up," said Fitz to Reilly. "I'm just pleased I won't be around to witness it."

"You've no idea how much better that makes me feel," replied Reilly. "I'd hate to think what you'd do to me once you had me on the slab."

They all found the banter amusing. Fitz asked Gardener what they had discovered to date and Gardener explained.

"And it's definitely the same man?" inquired Fitz.

"It would seem that way," replied Gardener.

"And he had a wife in Bursley Bridge, and a mistress in Bramfield that he was planning on taking to Portugal to live? Those towns are quite close to each other, how did all three never meet?"

"We don't know that they didn't," said Gardener.

"Sounds like an interesting situation," said Reilly. "But no one's admitting to anything."

"How could he afford to live in Portugal if he was only a delivery driver?" asked Fitz.

"It would appear that his wife was well off," said Gardener.

"If that's the kind of bloke Challenger is," said Reilly, "then maybe he was going to sell the family home without Grace knowing."

"Are you going to delve into his financial situation?" asked Fitz.

"That's about the only thing we can do," said Gardener. "The problem we have is that Davey Challenger is missing, and we have a body in a burnt-out van. We need to know whether it is the same man. Until then, we can't do a great deal."

"Davey Challenger could walk back into either woman's life at any moment," said Reilly.

"So is there anything more you can tell us," asked Gardener, "about the man in the van?"

"Not as much as I'd hoped for," said Fitz, consulting his computer, and then his notes from a folder on his desk. "Your man was definitely dead before the fire in the van was started. I think we already established that at the scene."

Fitz pulled out another sheet of paper.

"We did find traces of an accelerant on the clothing. I called Roy Dodgson – the man with the sniffer – this morning. He's already been over and taken samples, so that might be of some use."

"Do you know *how* he was killed, or when?" asked Gardener.

"As for the 'when'," said Fitz, "it must have been at some point during the early hours of Saturday morning. You mentioned the wife had last seen him at seven-thirty on the Friday night. Depending on where he went from there you might get a later sighting. As you know, it's not an exact science, so for now we'll have to settle for somewhere between seven-thirty on Friday night, and six o'clock on Saturday morning."

"Any idea on how, then?" asked Reilly.

Fitz shook his head. "That's still a bit of a mystery too. There are no wounds on the body at all to suggest anything external has happened."

"Which means you have to start looking internally," said Gardener.

"Which also suggests that this might be premeditated," said Reilly.

"Possibly," replied Fitz. "The degree of burning wasn't too intense. There may still be signs of poison or drugs in the bloodstream. I've taken samples and sent them off for toxicology, gentlemen, and I've requested a fast-track DNA. I should be able to let you know more quite soon."

"How soon?" Reilly asked.

"Maybe tomorrow," replied Fitz. "But as today is Sunday, I can't guarantee anything."

Gardener passed over the two bags containing personal items that the wife and the girlfriend had supplied.

"Can you fast-track those as well?"

"I take it these belong to our man leading the double life?"

"Yes," said Gardener. "Hopefully, those will confirm if the man in the van is Davey Challenger." Gardener rose from his chair. "Okay, Fitz, we'll leave you in peace. Anything planned for the rest of your day?"

"A visit to the shops now he's been here," said the pathologist, glancing at Reilly.

"Any chance you can find any of those nice chocolate Boost bars for tomorrow?" asked the Irishman. "I'm very partial to those."

"Doesn't his wife feed him?" Fitz asked Gardener.

"I think so," said Gardener, "along with everyone else."

As Gardener headed for the door, he turned and asked Fitz, "Didn't find any jewellery on the man in the van, did you?"

Fitz glanced upwards. "Jewellery? No."

Chapter Fourteen

Across Monday lunchtime, Gardener and Reilly opened the door to the incident room and slipped inside, surprised to find only Bob Anderson and Frank Thornton waiting for them.

"Welcome back. Good to see you both," said Gardener, closing the door and crossing the room to the whiteboards. He checked his watch. "Where are the others?"

The rest of the team filed in; each and every one of them was dressed in scene suits, gloves, booties and masks. On the front of Dave Rawson's suit was a big red cross and the word 'unclean' had been drawn.

Reilly doubled over with laughter. Gardener couldn't help himself, either. Anderson and Thornton turned.

"You set of bastards," shouted Anderson, and the whole room erupted into laughter.

Once it died down and the scene suits were removed, Gardener allowed them five minutes of banter before starting the meeting.

For the sake of Anderson and Thornton, Gardener recapped everything they had found since Saturday morning, using the whiteboards and crime scene photos.

He then explained where he and Reilly had been, and reported back on how differently the missing man was described by Grace Challenger and Monica Rushby.

"Is it definitely the same man?" asked Anderson.

"Yes," said Gardener, passing around the photos that he had taken from both women.

"Creep," said Sarah Gates.

"How do you do that?" asked Julie Longstaff. "The more I hear about people like him, the more I appreciate being single."

"Do you think either of the women knew about the other one?" asked Thornton.

"My gut feeling is no," said Gardener.

"It certainly brings into question why he was killed," said Sharp.

"Assuming the man in the van *is* Davey Challenger," said Gardener. "We could be barking up the wrong tree."

"Maybe it isn't him at all. It's possible," offered Sharp, "that he had more than two women on the go, and now he's with the third."

"Good point, Colin," said Gardener. "Which is why we need to concentrate our efforts on the body in the van. We can't think about Challenger's position until we can prove whether he is the victim of the fire or not."

"What's your gut feeling, sir?" asked Cragg.

Gardener thought about the question. "Not sure. I still feel that we have to pursue the missing persons as we would any other, until we know more. See if Challenger's bank accounts have been used since he was last seen. There are other things we can do but I'll come back to that. We need to discuss Fitz's findings first. Then I can issue some tasks."

"What did Fitz have to say?" asked Cragg.

"He's confirmed a little of what we already suspected; that the victim was dead before the fire started. Interestingly, there were no external wounds to suggest that the gun inside the van had been used, either on the victim or anyone else."

"What does he think killed him, then?" asked Gates.

"It's obviously something internal," said Reilly. "Fitz doesn't know, so he's collected some samples and sent them off."

"Along with photographs," said Gardener, "we also collected toothbrushes and hairbrushes from both women and gave them to Fitz for a fast-track DNA, which will prove one way or another whether it is Challenger in the van. Bearing that in mind, I take it we've had no sign of Challenger yet."

"I've not heard anything," said Cragg, "but I do have something interesting that you *will* want to hear."

"Go on," said Gardener.

"May I?" asked Cragg, pointing to the front of the room.

Gardener moved aside. "Be my guest."

Cragg stepped up to the front and spread the contents of his file on a table.

"I got to thinking about the gun, so I went back to *our* files. I think I've found something that we need to take seriously.

"Starting in December, we've seen a series of post office robberies carried out in the area. The first one was in Thirsk, Market Place. They picked a perfect day, Saturday the 18th, market day, week before Christmas. The town was busy, people all over the place, parting with their hard-earned cash. Some of the traders had already deposited money in the post office.

"Right on the point of closing, a large black van drew up opposite, on the market square itself. Two men calmly exited and slipped inside the post office quietly so as not to arouse too much attention. They wore masks and gloves. Only the postmaster, Duncan West, and a female colleague, Jean Simpson, were working at the time. The postmaster said they were closing and looked up from what he was doing. One of them drew a baseball bat from his sleeve and struck the man.

"Jean Simpson screamed as the other produced a knife and a bag, threatened her, and told her to put the cash in the bag. West were out cold, and bleeding. Worried sick, she complied, after which they tied her up and then calmly walked out. Equally as calmly, they crossed the road, jumped in the van and drove away quietly, so as no one knew what were really happening.

"Alarm was only raised when a Christmas shopper by the name of Andrea Marchant, a resident of Thirsk, needed some extra cards, and thought it odd that the lights were still on in the post office at six o'clock."

"There were no guns involved?" questioned Gardener.

"Not on the first one," replied Cragg.

"Any witnesses?" asked Reilly.

"Not many that actually witnessed anything," replied Cragg. "It was all pretty calmly done so reports were a bit thin on the ground. By the time it had happened, the market traders had either already gone, or were in the process of packing up and leaving."

"Did we get a description?" asked Sharp.

"Two men, one around average height and build, the other a bit on the heavy side, but neither were recognised from that. Most witness statements were the same."

"What about CCTV?" asked Longstaff.

"Picked out the registration plate."

"But still no result, obviously," said Reilly.

"If you had the registration, why couldn't you find the van?" asked Sharp.

"Here's the interesting bit, until a week previous, the van had belonged to a potato merchant from Middlesborough, believe it or not. When we spoke to him, he said it had been sold for scrap. But the new keeper had not registered anything. As much as we tried, we drew a blank with the new keeper and the van. Bloody thing just vanished after the robbery."

Cragg took a sip of his drink and consulted his notes further.

"We had all the usual suspects on file and checked them out. Jimmy Banks lives on the far side of Armley, been in and out of the prison so often that that's his business address now. But he fries bigger fish than this. Andrew Rodmell in Farsley, he's already inside doing a six-years stretch for the same thing. Bill Sanderson, who actually lives in Thirsk, had an alibi but was well pissed off that someone had done the town he lived in and he knew nothing about it."

That comment raised everyone's spirits.

"None of them were responsible, so we assumed – rightly or wrongly – that it was a new gang," said Cragg.

"Manny Walters wasn't involved in this, was he?" laughed Reilly.

"You're joking, aren't you?" replied Cragg. "Too rich for his tastes, anyway, he's turned over a new leaf, after all that business with Robbie Carter. He's come into money, but nobody will tell us how. Rumour has it he found and sold a very expensive camera worth quite a few quid."

"Found it where?" asked Paul Benson.

"No idea," said Cragg. "But it won't have been anywhere legal, will it?"

Gardener recollected the case and asked, "Any news of Robbie Carter?"

Cragg shook his head. "Still missing."

"He'll turn up," said Reilly. "They always do."

Gardener jotted a few notes on a clean whiteboard and then turned back to Cragg.

"Okay, Maurice, the floor's all yours. Let's hear more."

Chapter Fifteen

Cragg sorted through his files again.

Gardener was quite amused that the older man had taken the floor and was chairing the meeting. It must have been some years since he'd done that.

"The Square on Maltongate in Thornton le Dale," said Cragg. "Monday, January 24th. It's part of Wardill Bros, which is a newsagent and general store. It's very pleasant, opposite a large green, with plenty of trees, benches, and a cenotaph."

"A what?" asked Patrick Edwards.

"A war memorial, son. It's usually a statue of a soldier, where the dead are remembered."

Edwards blushed, as if he should have known, or perhaps shown a little more respect.

Cragg continued. "It was the same thing. They're open till six, but the post office closes at five-thirty. It was quiet because it were January. Very few people milling around, and the procedure were almost identical. They parked up very quietly outside the shop in the parking area, calmly walked in wearing masks and gloves, produced a baseball bat, and a bloody machete."

"A machete," repeated Reilly. "Christ, they meant business this time."

"Was it the same van?" asked Gardener.

"No," said Cragg, "I'll come to that in a minute. There were two customers in the shop, both of whom told exactly the same story when questioned. The robbers told them to keep calm, keep your mouth shut, do as we ask, and nobody will get hurt."

"Easy to say when you're holding a machete," said Rawson.

"Did anyone get hurt?" asked Gardener.

Cragg shook his head. "One of the robbers then locked the door, whilst the other collected all mobiles and left them on one of the shelves. The customers were not asked to give up anything they had, money or otherwise. The customers and the staff were all ordered behind the post office screen. One of the staff were asked to get the money from the tills and the safes while everyone else were tied up. When they had the money, the last one was tied up. On this occasion no one were harmed. And again, they quietly walked out of the shop and drove away."

"Sounds like a professional outfit," said Reilly.

"They knew what they were doing," said Longstaff. "They'd obviously watched the place."

"For how long, I wonder," said Gates. "It's odd that little communities like this are being watched and targeted and it all goes unnoticed. Everyone usually knows everyone in villages and small towns."

Gardener agreed, and then asked, "Witnesses?"

"They all said the same thing," replied Cragg. "So we figured it was the same two people. One of them never spoke. The one who did, there were nothing special about his voice."

"What about the van?" Gardener asked.

"CCTV once again recorded the details, and exactly the same thing had happened. It came from a garage in Haxby near York. It had been used as a delivery van and had come to the end of its life. A trader bought it, claimed he had a use for it, but it was never registered, and neither have been seen since."

Gardener made notes on the whiteboard.

"Couldn't really see a pattern," said Cragg. "It wasn't market day because Thornton le Dale doesn't have one, and they hit the place on a Monday."

"It's definitely the same gang," said Rawson. "They know what they're doing, they're in and out fast and leave in a puff of smoke."

"I assume there is a third," said Gardener. "Did a pattern emerge then?"

"The only pattern that's showing up," said Cragg, "is that it happens once a month. The next one was February, Park Square in Masham. Once again it's a newsagent, and a one-man operation at that; perfect place for it. Nice long parking area outside; closes at five o'clock. Market day in Masham is the first Sunday of every month, but they hit this place on Wednesday the 16th, and closing time was six, so still not much of a pattern. Being February, it was still dark; tea-time, no one were around. Same MO: they drove the van calmly in, a grey Transit, baseball bat and a machete again. The shopkeeper, Rupert Grimes, simply did as they asked him. It was definitely the same gang. No violence used, said to just put the money in, say and do nothing and no harm would come to him.

"Once again, only one of them spoke. The other collected the shopkeeper's mobile and tied him up afterwards, and he remained there until eight o'clock when a local, a Mrs Wilma Morrison, noticed the lights were still on and went to investigate. Police were called. CCTV in the shop showed us what had happened but neither of the men looked like anyone we knew.

"CCTV registered the van plates as belonging to a shopkeeper here, in Bramfield. You'll not believe it, but it was the bloke who'd taken over old Armitage's shop, used it as a delivery van, but it was sold on and no details were given, or they couldn't be confirmed. They were false, and the van disappeared."

"I wondered what had happened to Armitage," said Gardener.

"All that business with his nephew finished him. Rumour has it he never stepped in the shop again after that. Sold it lock, stock and barrel."

"Can't say I blame him," said Gardener.

"So we have absolutely no idea about the vans or the new keepers?" said Reilly. "Each one had been bought, used for one job, and then disappeared?"

"Seems that way," said Cragg. "They certainly haven't been sold on or we would have known."

"Well what the hell happened to them?" asked Rawson.

"If they'd been scrapped," said Gardener, "the DVLA would have a record, so maybe we should look at that, just in case."

"Yes," said Longstaff. "Maybe whoever had them allowed the heat to die down and *then* scrapped them."

"Maybe someone has a barn full of them," said Gates.

"Good point, Sarah," said Gardener. "Perhaps we should keep our eyes open when we're travelling around here. We just might come across them. It's also possible that they've been sold again for scrap, and perhaps crushed."

"Wouldn't there be an anomaly in the records?" asked Cragg. "If they hadn't been registered but were then sold on after the robbery, there would be a discrepancy."

"Possibly so, Maurice," said Gardener. "But until now they haven't been a part of our inquiry, and they still may not be. Whoever was investigating this case might be able to share something with us. So where are we going with all this, Maurice? You obviously believe that there is a connection to our van fire."

"Yes, sir. I think they are connected, because it's possible that the van used previously in robbery number three may well have been used again in number four – along with the gun you found in the burning van. And this time, it were a totally different ball game."

Chapter Sixteen

"Where was this one?" Gardener asked.

"Here," said Cragg.

"Here?" repeated Gardener.

Cragg nodded. "Well, not Bramfield, but up the road in Bursley Bridge."

"And you believe that the gun in our van fire may have been used in the fourth robbery?" asked Gardener.

"Maybe even the van," said Cragg. "Though we don't have any evidence of it being used as yet."

"Okay, Maurice," said Gardener. "We'd better have the details."

"The post office is in Market Place, sandwiched between The Bay Horse Inn and what used to be the National Westminster Bank. It's part of Moreland's newsagents and closes at four on a Friday, which is when they struck."

"Last Friday?" asked Gardener.

Cragg nodded and continued. "Parking is available right outside, but by all accounts, they parked in the pub car park next door, The Bay Horse, which has a bit of a back alley between the two buildings, and it has a rear access – so it were perfect. Drive in one way, and out the other.

"Once again, they calmly left the van – masked up – and strolled into the shop. What sets this robbery apart from the others is that *both* men had guns, *both* men were threatening, but neither one appeared to want to use the gun."

"And we're sure it was the same men?" asked Reilly.

"From what we've pieced together, we believe so," said Cragg. "However, a third party – another man with a gun – suddenly appeared from nowhere, taking everyone by surprise, including the two robbers that were already in there.

"One of them questioned the third man, but he told them to shut up, and fired a warning shot as if to prove he were in charge. The original two robbers immediately fled the scene through the front door, empty-handed.

"Then he pointed his gun at the postmaster and told him to get the cash in the bags. The two customers in the shop feared for their lives; they had no idea what was going on. The postmaster put the money in the sacks but when he came around the counter to hand it over, he made the mistake of trying to overpower the third man."

"Oh, Jesus," said Reilly. "I'm guessing this didn't end well for him."

"Not really. The gun went off and all hell broke loose. The robber told everyone to hand over their phones and left quickly, through the back door."

"The gun went off?" asked Gardener. "Was anyone injured?"

"The postmaster," replied Cragg. "His name is George Spencer. The bullet hit him in the shoulder and he crashed back into a stand and split his head open. It was a right mess."

"So what happened next?" asked Sharp. "It can't have ended there."

"One vehicle in the back of the pub car park was identified - a Transit van. This time it was a red one, an ex-post office van, which had previously ended its life at the post office in Liverpool. It went to an auction, where it was sold, but the details given were false and the van disappeared until it were used in the robbery, and then disappeared again. The man who bought it did not fit the description of either of our original robbers so it's possible the third man were involved in that."

"Any CCTV?" asked Gardener.

"Yes," replied Cragg. "CCTV shows him leaving the premises and making off through the back. Cameras picked him up running through Burgate a few minutes later, and later still, walking calmly through Castlegate. The interesting thing here is, he'd dropped or dumped his package somewhere and he'd changed his top. The trousers and boots were the same, but we suspect he ditched the mask and put on a hoodie so as not to attract attention and not be seen by cameras. But we couldn't see any trace of a vehicle. We presume he used one, but we have no idea where he hid it."

"He must have had a vehicle," said Gates.

Longstaff agreed. "You don't rob a post office with a gun on foot, do you?"

"So we have no idea what the third party was driving or where he was parked," said Reilly. "It's a bit of a stretch, but you're thinking it's just possible it could be the van that was set on fire."

Cragg nodded. "It's possible."

"So what happened to the postmaster?" asked Gardener.

"He was taken to St James's hospital in Leeds. His name's George Spencer. A widower, lives in Bursley Bridge, no family, worked for the post office all his life. He was in a coma when he reached the hospital and he's still in one now."

"So no one has been able to speak to him?" inquired Anderson.

"I'm afraid not," replied Cragg. "I check regularly, but he's not come round, and the doctors are afraid he might never recover."

"That makes it robbery with violence," said Gardener. "Who's investigating this?"

"A man called Wilkinson, Harrogate CID. All the robberies apart from this one happened on his patch."

"Can you find me his details, Maurice?" asked Gardener. "We'll need to speak to him, especially if these two cases are connected."

Cragg nodded.

"The interesting thing here is the change of pattern," said Gardener. "No one injured in the first three, but the postmaster in the last one?"

"It does sound like the original robbers were taken by surprise," said Anderson. "They had planned to rob the place and someone else took over, someone they didn't expect to be there."

"Why the guns?" said Benson. "The previous robberies did not involve guns, but the fourth did. Were they planning to use them, or just frighten people?"

"What about witness statements?" asked Gardener.

"Pretty much as it was described to you," said Cragg.

"Were the descriptions of the original robbers the same as the first three?" asked Gardener.

"Yes," replied Cragg.

"So who was the third robber?" asked Gardener.

"Is it the victim in the burnt-out van?" asked Reilly.

"That could be something to think about," said Gardener. "Did we get any details of the bullet from the gun fired at the postmaster?"

"Yes," said Cragg. "Ballistics believed it came from a sawn-off 20-bore."

That silenced the room for a few seconds.

"So there is a possibility that the gun in our van is the gun used in the fourth post office robbery," said Gardener.

"And it could also mean that the *man* in our van was the surprise third robber, and this was payback?" said Reilly.

"Possible," said Gardener. "Leaving the gun may have been a message. After all, whoever removed the serial number would know we would struggle to trace it back to anyone."

"Still leaves the question of who it is in the van," said Sharp.

"Is it Challenger?" asked Gates.

"If it is," said Gardener, "we need to know a lot more about him."

Gardener shuffled over to Cragg and browsed through his paperwork.

"This is going to be very uncomfortable for Grace Challenger, especially if it turns out to be her husband."

Gardener picked up a pen and updated the whiteboard. Once done, he turned.

"Before I get into actions, can you guys quickly update me on anything else you've found today?"

Chapter Seventeen

Gates and Longstaff went first, reporting that they knew a little more about the van but probably nothing constructive yet. Their last hope was that the ECU had not suffered any fire damage, so that Ford could successfully download the information, which was due to take place tomorrow.

"So what's the bit you do know?" asked Gardener.

"We managed to scour what we could of the front section for prints," said Gates.

"We took them from the steering wheel and the inside of the cab," said Longstaff. "We're running them through the system but, as yet, no hits."

"But considering what Sergeant Cragg has just told us," said Gates, "we may be able to get in touch with the last official owner and see if we can have his prints for elimination purposes."

"Good idea," said Gardener.

"Unless he's involved," offered Reilly. "Might not be so keen, then."

"Another good point," said Gardener. "Okay, ladies, keep on it. I'd certainly be interested to hear what Ford find out. That could move things along very nicely."

Further house-to-house inquiries had yielded nothing. No one had reported seeing any unusual activity in or around the town, and particularly not involving strangers. Nor could anyone say anything further about the fire.

There was no news on the accelerant, which they felt was like trying to find a needle in a haystack. Roy Dodgson had discovered the chemical signature and was now setting about the arduous task of trying to find exactly where it had come from but, as Gardener said, it could be anywhere. There were an awful lot of petrol stations in the UK alone; and that was assuming it had been bought recently. It was always possible it could have been stored in a jerrycan in someone's barn for years.

Gardener glanced at Thornton and Anderson. "I think I'm going to task you guys with finding out who was in the van. That means looking at DNA in particular. I'm really hoping Fitz will have something tomorrow.

"Facial recognition would help but from what we've seen of the victim, there wasn't much of his face left. However, I want all of you to take copies of Challenger's photo and ask around. Somebody somewhere will remember something about him. He will have been seen, and even though most of the locals will know him, it's possible he was seen doing something out of character."

He glanced at Benson and Edwards. "Dental records will be worth chasing, so contact Fitz and see if he can help you out. From there, you can comb the dentists. Visit the village of Morton and see what you can pick up on Challenger? Take the photos. If he really did live there or rented a place, someone will know. Definitely check out the address that Monica Rushby gave us the night he left her in the car. Check his bank records to see if there has been anything withdrawn since he was last seen."

"I've just had a thought," said Anderson. "You mentioned the locals. What if this isn't an outside gang? What if it *is* someone local?"

"Yes," said Thornton, "if they were local, they would blend in. No one would bother about them if they saw them every day."

Gardener nodded, turning to Cragg. "Maurice, can we have everything on the local bad boys that you mentioned earlier, and any others you can think of?"

Cragg nodded. "Consider it done."

"Despite all of that," said Gardener, turning back to Anderson and Thornton, "I still have a feeling about Challenger, and I think for the time being it's worth making him the number one priority, despite there being no guarantee that it's him in the van. Check his work colleagues, contacts and especially the darts team at the pub. The clues are there: he's been missing since Friday and the final robbery used an ex-post office van. If it turns out to be Challenger in the van, then we're halfway there. If it isn't we'll hand it over to Wilkinson and continue with what we're supposed to be doing."

"What are you thinking, boss?" Reilly asked.

"That something has gone wrong. The vans used in the first two robberies appeared to have disappeared. For some reason the third maybe didn't. Let's assume that whatever the original gang did with the first two –

scrapped them, torched them, sold them abroad – they didn't do with the third."

"Maybe there's more people involved in this operation," said Reilly, "and one of them got greedy."

"Instead of scrapping the van," said Rawson, "or torching it, maybe they hid it and then sold it on for whatever reason."

"The only reason I can think of," said Anderson, "is that someone *did* get greedy and started double-crossing the others, which is dangerous – hence the body in the van."

"But how did Challenger become involved?" asked Gates. "He seems like a simple postman."

"Unless he's been involved all along and he's the greedy one," said Longstaff.

Gardener conceded that point and then glanced at Sharp and Rawson.

"I'd like you two to go and speak to Grace Challenger. See if she knows where he was on the nights of the previous robberies. If he wasn't at home, we need to know where he was. We need to know if he was involved in any of the robberies."

"We'd better pay a visit to the girlfriend as well," said Sharp. "See if *she* knows where he was on those nights."

"Okay," said Gardener. "And speak to Roy Dodgson, see if anything comes up with the accelerant."

Gardener wrote the notes on the whiteboard and then addressed Cragg.

"Maurice, I know it's a long shot, but can we contact the previous owners of the vans that we know of, and see if there are any photos of the trader, or traders, who bought them? CCTV might help, if they have it."

Cragg nodded.

Gardener then addressed Gates and Longstaff.

"If there *is* time, either before or after you've met with Ford, can you check out the CCTV that Maurice has on the van robberies, particularly the fourth in Bursley

Bridge? You never know, a fresh pair of eyes just might pick up on something.

"I think that's about all for now," said Gardener.

Chapter Eighteen

Gardener and Reilly had arranged to meet Tom Wilkinson, from Harrogate CID, in Russell's café on Market Place, on the opposite side of the road to the Bay Horse Inn, close to Moreland's newsagent and the main post office. Reilly stood outside of Russell's for ten minutes staring into the window and making a list of all the pies and pastries he wanted to try before leaving and saying that he *would* return should he not manage the task. Gardener had no doubts about that.

They entered the shop to find a long counter on the right. A few people were seated, and Reilly ordered drinks for them both. The man sitting with his back to them at the first table was Wilkinson, with a fresh cuppa and a Danish.

Gardener flashed his warrant card and introduced himself. Wilkinson stood and shook his hand, glancing at Gardener's hat.

"Nice," he said. "It's the type of hat that shows a man means business. Where did you get it?"

"My late wife bought it for me," said Gardener, which was probably the first time he had given anyone a true explanation.

"I'm sorry," said Wilkinson, leaving it at that.

Wilkinson was equally as tall as Gardener, and also sported a short back and sides haircut that was mostly black, but greying at the temples. He seemed older, and stockier. He was wearing a dark blue suit with a white shirt and blue tie and black leather shoes, and his accent suggested he was local. Gardener had the impression he was an old-school officer, a man who probably wasn't afraid to take a risk but usually achieved his results going by the book.

Reilly appeared with a tray, on which he had tea and coffee, accompanied by a croissant and a sausage roll.

"A man after my own heart," said Wilkinson, shaking hands with the Irishman after he had put the tray on the table.

"Man needs to eat," said Reilly.

"Couldn't agree more," said Wilkinson, before glancing at his own plate. "Hence the Danish."

"Oh, no," said Gardener, "not another one. I'm surprised there's any food left in Bursley Bridge."

All three men laughed and once the pleasantries were over, Gardener said, "I appreciate you meeting us here. Hopefully we didn't disturb you from what you were doing."

"Not at all," said Wilkinson. "In fact, I was already in the town conducting a follow-up interview with the staff. It's amazing how things come back to you after a day or so, but you'll know that."

Gardener agreed before explaining the case they were investigating, in quite some detail. He then asked if Wilkinson would tell them what *he* knew.

Wilkinson took them through the post office robberies, what exactly happened, and how the fourth robbery was a little different because of another masked raider with a shotgun.

"Did you know the gun was fired twice?" Wilkinson asked Gardener, who nodded, then continued.

"We believe the first time was by mistake. We don't think the newcomer meant to fire it, he was a bit overexcited and simply wanted to assert his authority. The bullet blew a hole in the wall to the left of one of the original robber's head." Wilkinson grabbed his pad from an inside pocket and opened it to the relevant page. "He then shouted, and I quote, 'Fuck this for a lark.' The pair of them left the scene immediately."

"They didn't fire any shots?" questioned Gardener.

"No," said Wilkinson. "One gun going off must have been too much for them."

"If you can't stand the heat, get out of the kitchen, comes to mind," said Reilly.

"Did anyone recognise the voice of the original robber?" asked Gardener.

"No."

"The bullet you dislodged from the wall," said Reilly, "and the one fired at the postmaster both came from a 20-bore shotgun?"

"Yes," replied Wilkinson. "Sawn off by all accounts."

Reilly glanced at Gardener, who nodded. "We believe we have the shotgun."

"Where did you find it?" asked Wilkinson.

"It was in the van that had been torched," said Gardener. "So we can sign that out for you and see if you can match bullet and gun."

"That would be helpful," replied Wilkinson. "Thank you."

"We also have a feeling that the van that was torched may have been used in the third robbery," said Reilly.

"How badly damaged is it?"

"Pretty bad," said Gardener. "Someone had done their best to remove everything that would identify it, but we have one or two tricks up our sleeves."

"You will let me know what you find, won't you?" asked Wilkinson.

Gardener nodded, and then asked, "Going back to the robbery, did any of the staff recognise any of the robbers?"

"The first time I interviewed them, they said they didn't," replied Wilkinson. "However, the second interview in the shop, less than an hour ago, revealed something new.

"Only two of them are still employed there. They already have a new postmaster, a Welshman by the name of Bryn Roberts. He couldn't really tell us anything. The other staff member who was there on the day, Sandra Pearson, has left. She feared it was too dangerous to carry on working there, despite the fact that it was unlikely the same gang would rob the same post office twice. But she had an answer for that; it wouldn't stop another gang trying it on."

"Can't fault that logic," said Reilly.

Wilkinson laughed. "I suppose you're right. Anyway, one of the girls, Gillian Westmoreland, this morning admitted she thought she did recognise the third man. She didn't recognise the others."

"Why didn't she say this on Friday?" asked Reilly.

"I can understand it," said Wilkinson. "She claimed she wasn't sure. She says this man actually works for them, and he'd always been nice to her, and she couldn't believe it of him. Nor did she want to get him into trouble if she was wrong."

"So why the change of heart?" asked Gardener.

"It's been preying on her mind over the weekend, and now that he's gone missing, she thought it might be important."

"That missing man wouldn't be Davey Challenger, would it?" asked Gardener.

Wilkinson nodded.

"Why does she think it was him?" asked Reilly.

"The eyes gave it away," said Wilkinson. "Apparently, Challenger has piercing blue eyes. No mistaking them."

Gardener thanked Wilkinson for his time, and they agreed between them that for the next few incident room meetings they should have a SPOC, a single point of contact, from each team so they could share information.

After leaving the café, Gardener called Sharp to inform him of the new development, and to tread carefully when interviewing Grace Challenger.

Chapter Nineteen

Colin Sharp was not surprised when Grace Challenger asked that he and Rawson remove their shoes at the door. His boss had told him about their visit. Instead of showing them through to the living room however, she led them straight into the kitchen where she made tea and provided biscuits.

The kitchen was at the back of the house and ran the entire width of it. The view of the expansive garden was pleasurable. Sharp noticed a summer house on one side, with a gazebo on the other. The room itself was homely, decorated with antique jars on shelves. On another shelf were a number of books and when Sharp leaned in closer, he noticed every one of them was a cookery book written by Nigel Slater.

Across the draining board, in a plastic container were freshly picked vegetables, and slotted around the kitchen in vases were fresh flowers. The room was spotless, much like the owner of the house who was dressed in a long, sleek, tight-fitting blue dress that reached her ankles and showed every curve to perfection. Grace's make-up was flawless.

"How can I help you, officers?" she asked.

"We'd like to ask some follow-up questions about your husband, Mrs Challenger," said Sharp.

"Have you found him?" she asked, hopefully. "Please tell me that he's okay, that it's not him in that van."

"Not yet," said Sharp. "I take it he hasn't shown up, or contacted you in any way?"

"Not a word," replied Grace, deflated. "Have you still not found out who the man in the van fire is?"

"We are following a number of lines of inquiry," said Sharp. "But sorry, as yet, we haven't."

"So it could still be my husband. Then again, it may not be, and that's something for me to cling on to," said Grace. "So what can I help you with?"

"You mentioned to my senior officer that your husband was out last Friday night."

"Yes, that's right. He left here about seven-thirty for a darts match."

"This may sound an odd question, Mrs Challenger, but do you know if he definitely made it to the match?"

"To be honest, no, I'm not sure he did. I have spoken to the landlord of the Rose Inn when I was contacting everyone my husband knew and I was trying to find him. He said there *was* no darts match."

"You didn't mention this to my boss," said Rawson.

"I'm sorry," replied Grace. "It must have slipped my mind."

"And you have no idea where he could have been?" asked Rawson.

"No. If he wasn't playing darts, what the hell *was* he doing?" said Grace, more to herself than Sharp and Rawson. "Whatever it was, it can't have been any good, can it? Because now he's gone missing."

Sharp consulted his notes. "You also mentioned that you hadn't been getting on of late."

"Well," said Grace, "every marriage has its ups and downs, we were just going through a bad patch, I suppose."

"And you indicated he had been quiet recently," said Rawson. "Do you have any idea what might have been on his mind?"

Grace fished a tissue out of a nearby box, her eyes tearing up.

"No, because he wasn't saying much. It could have been anything, maybe something to do with work. We live in terrible times, and you hear about all these cutbacks, and silly energy prices, maybe he was worried about that. But he had no need. We're comfortable."

Grace suddenly stopped and put the tissue down.

"Is there something you're not telling me?"

After pausing for thought, Sharp spoke. "The post office in the town was robbed on Friday, and we have reason to believe that your husband was involved."

Grace simply stared at the two detectives and Sharp found it very difficult to read her expression. She was obviously wrestling with what he had said.

Finally, she replied. "No. It's not possible, officers."

"One of the girls working in the shop thought she recognised him, Mrs Challenger," said Rawson.

"Pardon." Her face paled. "Are you trying to say my husband walked into a post office in broad daylight and robbed them, without wearing a mask? That's ridiculous. Everyone in this town knows him; he couldn't possibly have done that. And what did he hold them up with?"

"A sawn-off shotgun," said Sharp.

Grace opened her mouth and closed it without saying anything, but then she did speak.

"A shotgun? Are you serious? He doesn't own a shotgun. Where would he get a shotgun from? I think she has the wrong man, officers. My husband is not a violent man. He's never hurt anything or anyone in his life. I've seen him bring spiders in from the outside because it was cold."

That was a new one on Sharp, bringing them *in*.

"Besides," continued Grace, "he was at work."

"You know that for a fact?" asked Rawson.

"Well I don't know it for a fact, but where else would he be? There must be some mistake. She must have made a mistake."

Sharp pressed on. "Perhaps you could help us with something else."

"I'm still getting over the shock of my husband robbing a post office, are you trying to tell me there is more?"

"We have some dates, Mrs Challenger," said Rawson. "We wondered if you could help us with those. Maybe you can tell us where he was on these dates."

"What are they?" asked Grace.

"The first one is Saturday, 18 December."

Grace's expression said she was thinking about it. "Wait a minute." She left the kitchen and slipped into another room, quickly returning with two diaries. "I can't guarantee anything."

She opened it up and settled on the page. "I *can* help with that one. It was the week before Christmas. He was off work, and we both went Christmas shopping in York."

That pretty much took the wind out of Sharp's sails. It definitely gave Davey Challenger an alibi for the first robbery in Thirsk.

"Was he with you all day?"

Grace stared at him. "What kind of a question is that? Of course, he was."

"How did you get to York?"

"We took the train, from Bursley Bridge, about nine-thirty in the morning. The reason we did that was so we could have a meal out, and a drink, without the worry of driving."

"And you left York… when?"

"If I remember correctly, it would have been around five o'clock."

"What about Monday, 24 January?" asked Rawson.

Grace opened up another diary. "There's nothing in here, so he would have been working."

"Wednesday, 16 February?"

She leafed through more pages. "Working again. I'm sure you can check all these easily enough with his employer."

"We will, Mrs Challenger, and thank you for your time."

"I still can't believe it, officer," said Grace. "I just can't believe my husband robbed the post office here in the town, or any other post office for that matter."

Sharp could see no further reason to detain or question her. She had certainly given her husband an alibi for the first robbery. They would have to dig a little deeper for the others.

Grace saw them to the door.

"You will let me know if you find anything, won't you? This is all very unsettling. I really don't want to think he ended his life in such horrible circumstances – or that he's ended it at all."

* * *

An hour later they were leaving Monica Rushby's house; she could add nothing more to their plight. She had been at work herself on the dates of all the robberies, so she had not seen Davey Challenger at all.

Sharp phoned Bob Anderson and gave him the news, asking if he could confirm with Challenger's employer if he had been at work on the dates of the robberies.

Chapter Twenty

Two hours after the detectives had left, Grace busied herself like never before, in an effort to stop her mind from wandering, thinking unsavoury thoughts about the man she had married but who now appeared to be a stranger.

She had washed and peeled all the vegetables for her evening meal, and she had cleaned the pots, as well as the kitchen – though she hadn't needed to. Outside, she pruned the trees, plants and bushes that needed attention. She now found herself back at the kitchen table with a freshly brewed herbal tea, her diaries, and a pad and pen.

Who had she been married to?

Grace's head was a mess. Thoughts bounced around like they were inside a pinball machine.

She took a sip of her tea, feeling nauseous. If she was being honest, she knew he had not been the man she married, for quite some time.

Something her mother always told her about lying was that you can lie to anyone you like, but you cannot lie to yourself, so if she really was being honest, she knew about his infidelity. She knew he had been seeing someone else.

December in York had sewn those seeds of doubt. He had disappeared for ten minutes, both of them going to different shops. Grace had seen him in one of the jewellers in the town. She had been outside. He hadn't seen her. As she stared through the window, she noticed him buying an expensive pendant. They had even gift-wrapped it in blue paper with a silver bow.

But that present had never made it under their tree. In fact, she never saw it again.

As if that wasn't bad enough, she was presented with irrefutable evidence at the beginning of March when she had taken herself off to the Steam and Moorland Garden Centre on Bramfield Road. She needed to stock up for the summer ahead. Having spent some considerable time buying everything she needed, Grace had decided on a quick cuppa in the Engine Shed Restaurant before returning via one of the local farm shops to pick up something special for Davey's tea. He was very fond of steak, and she knew the place to buy it from.

But she never made it that far. She had spotted them both in the restaurant: her husband and a buxom blonde, laughing and joking. She also spotted the pendant, because the blonde was holding it out toward him.

Chapter Twenty-one

It was early Tuesday morning as Gardener assembled everyone into the briefing room for a catch-up. He'd managed to miss most of his officers the previous night and had only caught snippets of information. He needed a bigger picture.

He started by introducing them all to the SPOC, who turned out to be the man himself, Tom Wilkinson. Gardener asked him to brief the team with the news about the third man in the fourth robbery possibly being someone they wanted to talk to.

Once Wilkinson had finished, Gardener first asked Sharp and Rawson if they had anything to share on the accelerant.

"We spoke to Roy Dodgson last night," said Rawson. "In fact, it was quite late."

"He's pinned it down to a Shell service station in Birmingham," said Sharp.

"Birmingham?" questioned Gardener.

"Apparently," said Sharp. "Don't ask me how but he said he's managed to identify the signature and he knows it has come from a Shell station on New Street."

Gardener glanced at Cragg. "Outside gang?"

"From Birmingham?" said Cragg. "That doesn't make sense. Why come all *this* way to rob a post office?"

"Not much else about this case is making sense at the moment," said Gardener.

"We can check for robberies in and around the Birmingham area," said Wilkinson. "See if any of them were committed using the same signature."

"Okay," said Gardener, "but it does seem far-fetched. I can understand them robbing shops local to *them*, and maybe even within a fifty-mile radius, but not this far north."

"You'd be surprised," said Wilkinson. "Besides, they may not *be* from Birmingham."

Gardener conceded with a nod.

"There could be any number of reasons," continued Wilkinson. "They might be too well known in their own area. Perhaps someone new has joined the team; someone from this area."

"Okay," said Gardener. "We'll keep digging with that one." He turned to Sharp. "Can you liaise with Roy Dodgson, and speak to the Shell station on New Street? See if we can narrow it down to a date and, more importantly, is there any CCTV of the person who purchased it?"

"We might be lucky if whoever bought it used a credit card," offered Rawson.

"What are the chances?" asked Reilly. "These people will be strictly cash, I reckon."

"If we're really lucky," said Gardener. "He might have used a vehicle we can track, or maybe it was the Transit that's been set on fire."

"Instead of a jerrycan, you mean," said Reilly. "If he used a jerrycan, we may not see anything. He could have filled it up around the side of the van, out of view."

Gardener nodded, accepting the point his partner was making.

"At least we have *something* further to question," said Gardener. He glanced at Benson and Edwards. "Moving on, did you two get anywhere with Challenger?"

"We haven't managed the dentists yet," said Benson, "because we've only just got the records back from Fitz, but we'll try and tackle that today."

"We do have something from Morton," said Edwards. "The address he claimed to have lived at belongs to a young couple and they have never heard of him; they didn't even know he was their postman. We checked with Monica Rushby for the date of the weekend they were away, and believe it or not, the young couple who own the place were also on holiday."

"What are the chances of that?" said Longstaff.

"Pretty good," said Reilly. "He would probably have known that, especially as he delivers the mail."

"He'd have been in a bit of trouble if Monica had asked to go inside," said Benson.

"I'm quite sure he'd have had an excuse ready," said Gardener.

"But what the hell was he up to round the back of that couple's house?" asked Reilly.

"I doubt we'll ever find out, Sean, unless we find him alive and kicking, but even if he was up to no good it's too far back to start looking for any evidence for what we're investigating."

"I agree," said Thornton. "Chances are, whatever he was up to, he'll have covered his tracks since then."

Benson said they had spent the rest of their time showing Challenger's photo around the village of Morton.

"A lot of people knew him as the local postman; not many knew where he lived, but they knew he didn't live there."

"We came across that bloke who owns the scrapyard," said Edwards. "He lives in a right place."

"Derrick Mitchell," said Gardener. "He mentioned he lived around there when we spoke to him."

"It's an old chapel on Main Street, opposite the Spar shop and post office, of all things."

"The locals speak quite highly of him," said Benson. "Apparently he bought the building twelve years ago in an auction. The diocese had decided to sell due to lack of support and because it was falling into disrepair."

"He went head-to-head with a local builder," said Edwards. "He was never going to let the builder have it because he would have destroyed the character of the place, either by demolishing and rebuilding, or turning it into flats and charging an extortionate rent."

"Although he's not a local," continued Benson, "the people living there really appreciate what he's done. He loved the old building and wanted it for himself. It had a big car park, which Mitchell renovated into green land, and is now home to all sorts of wildlife. He has a real bond with the people."

"Okay," said Gardener. "Nice to hear someone is prospering. And all that from a scrapyard; didn't know it paid so well. Anyway, with regards to Challenger, until we can put him in the burnt-out van, keep going with the dental records and everything else we have. We really do need to find out the identity of the victim."

Gardener made a mental note to chase up Fitz to see if the results of the blood samples had come back. He then zeroed in on Gates and Longstaff and asked about the van.

"Good news," said Gates. "We met with Ford who had all the relevant software for extracting the information from the ECU."

"Well done," said Gardener. "What did we find?"

"We have a registration, date of manufacture, and where it was originally bought," said Longstaff. She turned to Cragg. "Turns out it *was* the van used in robbery number three. The plates came up as belonging to a shopkeeper here, in Bramfield, the bloke who'd taken over old Armitage's shop."

"So who bought the van from him?" asked Gardener.

"Whoever it was," said Gates, "they didn't give the correct name and address and it was never registered from that point on."

"Did he recognise the man who bought it?" asked Reilly.

"No," said Longstaff.

"Did he know where the man had come from to buy it?"

"Manchester, or so he claimed."

"So where the hell has it been since then?" asked Reilly.

"Well hidden," said Gardener. "A barn, maybe?"

"Had to have been," said Sharp. "If that van had belonged to a local trader here in Bramfield, it would have been well known."

"Maybe not," said Rawson.

"What do you mean?" asked Gardener.

"If the van *was* local, and well known, maybe it wasn't hidden," said Rawson. "After all, if anyone saw it driving around, would they think any different?"

Gardener nodded, accepting his point. "In that case, now we have the information we need, it's worth trawling the CCTV from Bursley Bridge and Bramfield to see if we can plot the movements of the van. If, as Dave says, it was local, and no one would think twice if they saw it around, maybe our robbers were hidden in plain sight, so to speak."

"Isn't that what always happens?" said Reilly.

Gates nodded. "Okay, we can get on with that now."

"What about the CCTV footage from the robberies?" Gardener asked. "Did you have the chance to check any of it?"

"We did," said Longstaff. "But we couldn't see anything that hasn't been spotted already."

"We looked more closely at the third robber in the last robbery," Gates said. "We compared the build to the photos of Challenger, and they do appear to be very similar."

"But here's the interesting bit," said Longstaff. "We do have a match on the prints."

"In our system?" asked Gardener.

"No," said Longstaff.

"What we meant was," added Gates, "the body in the van matches the prints on the steering wheel, and those on the inside of the cab."

"And on the gun that we found in the van," said Longstaff.

That comment pleased Wilkinson. "Looks like you don't have to sign it out, after all," he said to Gardener.

"I don't suppose we've managed to match up prints on the personal stuff we took from Grace Challenger and Monica Rushby, have we?"

"We're on with that now," said Longstaff. "Fitz had sent them back and we've only just been to sign them out of exhibits."

Chapter Twenty-two

Gardener updated the whiteboard and turned his attention to Anderson and Thornton, asking what they knew.

"We have made some headway," said Anderson.

"We know there was no darts match on the Friday night, the day of the robbery," said Thornton. "We also took a call from Colin who had been over to see Challenger's wife. She'd *also* discovered that herself."

"We know he wasn't with his girlfriend," said Gardener. "Not unless he spent the night in the hospital."

"We've spoken to his work colleagues, and one or two of the darts team," said Anderson. "The last time anyone can remember seeing him was on Wednesday night. There *was* a darts match then, and he was there."

"How did he seem?" asked Gardener.

"According to his teammates, distracted," said Thornton. "He lost his match miserably, didn't have much to say, barely had a drink; in other words, not his usual self."

"He obviously had something on his mind," said Gardener. "Did anyone talk to him about it or discover a reason why?"

"A couple of people asked him if he was alright," said Anderson. "He shrugged it off, said he was fine but tired; thought he had a cold coming on."

"I think it's fair to assume – with what we know – that he was definitely involved in the robbery, but what happened to him after that is still a bit of a mystery," said Gardener. "What bothers me is we can't actually put *him* in the van yet. Has anyone seen him *since* Friday?"

"No," said Anderson.

"Furthermore," said Thornton, "he was not at work on the day of the robbery. He didn't phone in sick and made no contact whatsoever. He simply did not turn up and has not shown up for work since."

"Did his employer try to contact him on the day, or since?" asked Gardener.

"Yes," said Anderson. "Challenger's phone was switched off on the day and has been since."

"Which suggests something happened," said Reilly. "Amongst the burnt-out electrical stuff in the van, we definitely didn't find a phone, did we?"

"Not that I know of," said Gardener. He turned to Gates and Longstaff. "Have we had a chance to go through the electrical stuff?"

Gates nodded. "We have, but nothing is retrievable."

"It's well knackered," said Longstaff.

"Okay," said Gardener. "It was worth a shot." He returned his attention to Thornton. "I don't suppose the employer called Grace, did he?"

"We called his employer and asked," said Thornton. "But like he said, it's not his job to chase people round. It's up to Challenger to report in."

"And being a driver down," said Anderson, "it put him under pressure to try to draft in other people."

Gardener thought about that, and about Challenger.

"Maybe he was with the gang of thieves."

"Maybe he was, and things got out of hand," said Reilly. "A major disagreement, which is why he ended up in the van."

"In a way," said Gardener, "I'm hoping now that it is."

"However," said Anderson, "his employer confirmed that he *was* at work on the dates of the previous three robberies."

"Meaning he had an alibi," said Gardener.

"Doesn't mean he wasn't involved," offered Reilly.

"True," said Gardener. "But why would he have been a sleeping partner on the first three, and in the thick of it on the fourth?"

"And possibly in an argument that cost him his life," added Benson.

"Only one person knows the answer to that," said Cragg, "and we're yet to find him."

"Any movement on his bank accounts?" asked Gardener.

"Nothing that we've found," said Thornton.

"Maybe he's gone completely underground," said Gardener. "Let's face it, if he has the money from the post office robbery, he wouldn't need to use his bank account, would he?"

"Or," said Reilly, "he's the victim in the van."

"We definitely need to tie this up," said Gardener, frustrated. "We'll go and see Fitz after we've finished here."

Gardener asked Sharp and Rawson how they had found Grace, and what their opinion of her was.

"On the surface," said Sharp, "Challenger and her seem to me like a complete mismatch."

"Agreed," said Rawson. "She looks like a fashion model, he's your average Joe in the street. I suspect the place they live in isn't down to him."

"That's the idea we got," said Reilly.

"Seems Grace was left some money from an aunt," said Gardener. "Maybe it was quite substantial, enough to buy a nice place and set them up."

"But not enough that one of them couldn't give up working," said Gates.

"It could have been," said Longstaff, "judging by what we've heard. Maybe he *wanted* to carry on working, because of what he was involved in."

"Perhaps he *was* involved in all the robberies," said Rawson, "and that's why they're living in splendour."

"You think Grace is in on it?" asked Reilly.

"I wasn't actually saying that," replied Rawson.

"It's a point we might have to consider," said Gardener. "Looks can be deceiving. Grace looks like butter wouldn't melt but what if she is the brains behind everything?"

"It wouldn't be the first time, would it?" said Anderson. "What was that bloody old Ealing film where a gang of them were hiding in this woman's house, planning a robbery, doing their best to make sure she didn't find out?"

"But she knew more than they did all along." Thornton laughed.

"*The Ladykillers*," said Gardener. "I only know that because it's one of my dad's favourites and we have to watch it every time it's on."

After the laughing died down, Sharp said, "So where is Challenger? Whichever way we look at it, he's still missing."

"Maurice," said Gardener, "you must know them both, what's your opinion?"

"From what I've seen – chalk and cheese. Grace is from out of town, York way, used to the finer things in life. Davey is a local boy, born and bred here. You very rarely see her but when you do, she's made up to the nines. I don't suppose any of that comes cheap. He's often in the town, in the pubs, as we've heard, playing darts. I saw them out for a meal once. She was dressed to kill, as usual, drinking wine, eating fine food. He was in jeans and a T-shirt, with a burger and a beer.

"But I will say one thing," continued Cragg, "I've never heard a drop of scandal anywhere, until I heard about him having a bit on the side. He doesn't have any form whatsoever, and neither does she for that matter. I'd be very surprised if she were involved."

"But not him?" asked Gardener.

"Of the two," replied Cragg, "I would say him rather than her. He's a lad about town, involved with the local crowds, more likely to have his finger in a few pies, or have his head turned by a lucrative offer. I checked out all the local gangs like you asked last time, but none of the usual names are involved."

"So that leaves us with an out-of-town gang, which could be likely given we're chasing a lead on the accelerant originating in Birmingham. Or, we have a new local gang, possibly in the shape of Challenger and his associates," said Gardener. "Just before we go, can we have someone on the previous owners of the vans used in the robberies? Are there any photos of the buyers from when the vans were sold on? Other than that, keep doing what you're doing. It's not easy but good old-fashioned detective work will be the key to this one. We're going to see Fitz. He may have something more. By the end of today I would really like to know the identity of the victim in the van so we can focus our investigation."

Chapter Twenty-three

Later in the day, Gardener and Reilly finally found Fitz in his office, sitting at his desk with his arms folded, staring into space. The heating was moderate, the lighting and the level of the music low.

"What have we got today, Fitz?" asked Reilly, heading for the coffee machine.

"Not enough for you, I should imagine."

"Oh come on now, don't be like that. If we didn't come and visit you, you'd have no one."

"If only," replied Fitz.

Reilly poured everyone coffee, which Fitz told him was salted caramel flavour.

Gardener rarely drank coffee, and never from a machine, but he made an exception for the coffee Fitz usually had.

"Where do you get all these flavours?"

"My wife. She knows all these little specialist places."

"Didn't manage to find a Boost bar, did she?" asked Reilly.

Fitz reached into a drawer and placed one on the desk. Reilly almost passed out as he lunged for it.

"I don't care what they say about you, none of it's true."

The phone shrilled and the pathologist answered. Gardener heard a one-sided conversation in which he detected that Fitz was up to his armpits in work.

"That bad?" asked Gardener, once he'd replaced the receiver.

"Strange one," he replied. "Three men found in a flat in Bradford. The doors were locked, the windows sealed. They were all in separate chairs, facing each other. The room was clock cold, looked like it had been that way for some time, and so had they. They're in here now; that was someone checking to see if I had found anything."

"Have you?"

"No," replied Fitz. "No idea what's killed them. There were no witnesses. They don't appear to have family, and about the only thing I can tell you is they look Asian, so whoever is investigating this one will have their hands full."

"Glad we're not," said Reilly.

"Ours isn't without its problems," said Gardener.

Fitz smiled. "I can clear up one of those for you."

"Go on," said Gardener.

"The man in the van is definitely Davey Challenger. The prints from the inside of the van, the gun, and the personal effects you gave me, all match. He is definitely your man."

"One problem down, another hundred to go," said Reilly. "At least we're going down the right path."

Gardener breathed a sigh of relief. That made things easier for him.

But not for Grace. He and Reilly would have to go and see her, and he had no idea how she would take it. In Grace Challenger he saw a desperate woman, underneath the surface. He suspected she was one of those people who lived life in their comfort zone. Despite all the bad things going on, so long as she had her house and her garden and her husband to cater to, everything was fine.

They were about to shatter that comfort zone.

"Well, that's one thing cleared up," said Gardener. "Are we any nearer to finding out what killed him?"

"Yes," said Fitz. "But you're probably not going to like it."

"When do we ever?" asked Reilly, finishing the last mouthful of the chocolate bar.

"We've had the samples back, and what we're looking at is a bit specialized, which is why I've drafted in some outside help."

"Christ," said Reilly. "If it's beyond you, I'm off now."

Fitz glanced past Gardener. "Ah, speak of the devil."

"Where have you been hiding, big boy," said a voice behind Gardener. He immediately blushed as he recognised who it was.

Vanessa Chambers walked around to Fitz's side of the desk. They had met on a couple of occasions. She was in her mid-thirties – blonde and bubbly with the most voluptuous figure and spoke with a confident upper-class accent. Vanessa was a botanist, and every bit as good as Fitz in her specialist subject.

She leaned forward. "The last time I saw you was in the centre of Leeds in the middle of a possible Hazchem scene. Pleased you managed to work your way out of it."

"So were we," said Reilly.

"How wonderful to see you both again."

Gardener nodded, a touch tongue-tied.

Vanessa poured herself a coffee before taking a seat. She was dressed in a tight-fitting white top, and an equally tight pair of black jeans.

"I've called Vanessa because of what we found in Challenger's body."

Reilly rolled his eyes. "What did I say about problems? Why don't we ever get easy cases?"

"You mean you'd prefer the one in Bradford?"

"Well, now you come to mention it. Do go on," he replied to Fitz.

The pathologist opened a file and scanned through it. "According to toxicology, we found traces of aconitine in his system, a substantial amount."

"Here we go," said Reilly.

"Oh dear," said Gardener. "What exactly is that?"

"It's a toxin," said Vanessa Chambers, "produced by the Aconitum plant – which is sometimes called the devil's helmet, or more commonly known as monkshood – which is notorious for its toxic properties. These plants are very popular. They're used quite a lot in traditional Chinese medicine. They still have some limited application in herbal medicine, but it's extremely difficult to calculate the appropriate dosage.

"It is barely soluble in water, but very soluble in organic solvents such as chloroform or diethyl ether. Aconitine is also soluble in mixtures of alcohol and water if the concentration of alcohol is high enough. Do you know," she said, "consuming as little as two milligrams of pure aconitine, or one gram of the plant itself, may cause death by paralyzing respiratory or heart functions? Toxicity can even occur through the skin; in other words, just touching the flowers can numb the fingertips."

Fitz took over, almost as if they were a double act.

"According to a review of different reports of aconitine poisoning in humans, quite a number of disturbing symptoms were observed, including neurological ones like paraesthesia and numbness of the face, as well as muscle weakness in the limbs. There are some cardiovascular symptoms too – hypotension, palpitations, and chest pains – as well as gastrointestinal ones, including nausea, vomiting, abdominal pain, and diarrhoea. It also causes dizziness, hyperventilation, sweating, difficulty breathing, confusion, headache, and lachrymation, which of course is, excessive tears.

"I have here a couple of reports of poisonings that have happened within the last three years, both in the General Infirmary in Leeds. Twenty-seven-year-old Katrina Williams of Yeadon developed some chest discomfort, dizziness, numbness, and weakness, one hour after taking a concoction of Chinese herbal medicines, which was found to contain nineteen components.

"She'd always enjoyed good health, with no history of cardiac disease. The herbal remnants were eventually examined, and one item did not match any of the herbs on the label; turned out to be a piece of Aconitum plant rootstock. Aconitine was detected in both the leftover herbal broth and the patient's urine. Her symptoms resolved completely in 24 hours with supportive therapy alone."

Vanessa Chambers also read from the file.

"Another case involved a forty-five-year-old lady called Lisa Thompson of Shipley near Bradford. She also became ill one hour after taking a herbal broth, which contained eleven ingredients, for a menstrual problem. She had the usual symptoms, which also improved with supportive treatment. Leftover herbal broth and a urine sample collected on the day of admission were analysed and aconitine was once again found in both."

"How long would it take for someone to die if they've taken a fatal dose?" asked Gardener.

"In a high dosage, not long," said Vanessa. "I take it you're referring to the van fire?"

Gardener nodded.

"It's hard to say when he was killed and when the van was set on fire," said Fitz. "But my guess is, he would have been dead within an hour of receiving the poison, so whoever you're looking for might just have a humane side to them."

"That's handy to know," said Reilly, "a murderer with a conscience."

"It suggests to me," said Gardener, "that the victim was probably killed somewhere else, dumped in the van, and then driven to the field to be torched?"

"As far as I have ascertained," said Vanessa, "the first symptoms of aconitine poisoning are usually within twenty minutes, but could take up to two hours following oral intake. These will include paraesthesia."

"What's that?" asked Reilly.

"Pins and needles," she replied. "Tingling, prickling. Sweating and nausea follow, which lead to severe vomiting, colicky diarrhea, intense pain and, finally paralysis of the skeletal muscles. Eventually, the victim will have a fatal heart attack."

"Have we found out how he'd ingested it?" asked Gardener.

"Not yet," said Fitz. "The victim's skin is badly burned, making it difficult to ascertain if it was internal or external."

Vanessa took over. "He could have been made to drink some liquid form of it or the plant could have been boiled down and crystallized and then produced in tablet form."

"Making this a highly specialized operation," said Gardener.

"I think it became specialized when he said aconitine," offered Reilly.

Fitz went into encyclopaedia mode. "Aconitine was the poison used by George Henry Lamson in 1881 to murder his brother-in-law in order to secure an inheritance.

"We also have evidence of it being used in 1953. Grigory Mairanovsky was a Soviet biochemist and poison developer. In experiments with prisoners in the secret NKVD laboratory in Moscow, he admitted killing around ten people using the poison."

"In 2004 a Canadian actor by the name of Andre Noble died from aconitine poisoning," added Vanessa. "He accidentally ate some monkshood while he was on a hike with his aunt in Newfoundland."

"How the hell can you accidentally eat that kind of stuff?" asked Reilly.

"Foraging can be dangerous. If you don't know what you're doing you could end up killing yourself."

"What does this stuff look like, and where do you find it?" asked Gardener.

"Now you're asking," said Vanessa. "It's a perennial herb often grown as an ornamental plant due to its attractive blue to dark purple flowers. All parts of the plant, especially the roots, contain toxins.

"It has been used since ancient times as a poison used on spears and arrows for hunting and battle," said Vanessa. "Ancient Romans used it as a method of execution.

"It is mainly native to western and central Europe where it is considered one of the most poisonous plants. Aconitine poisoning is rare in North America. When it does occur, it is generally due to confusion with an edible plant or unintentional ingestion by children.

"It's definitely most common in Asia due to the widespread use of herbal medications. In Hong Kong, aconitine is responsible for the majority of serious poisonings from Chinese herbal preparations.

"It's alleged that there are therapeutic uses, which include the treatment of joint and muscle pain. As a tincture applied to the skin, it is claimed to slow the heart rate in cardiac patients. Other claimed uses include reduction of fevers and cold symptoms."

"As we've said, gentlemen," continued Fitz, "in poisonings, the onset of symptoms occurs within minutes to a few hours after swallowing. The treatment is symptomatic and supportive; there is no specific antidote."

"There is a very low margin of safety between therapeutic and toxic doses of aconitine," added Vanessa.

Fitz closed his folder. "Sorry to add to your problems, gentlemen, but at least we know *what* killed him. You now need to find out who."

Reilly stood up. "I don't think you're sorry. If you were really sorry, you'd have given me another Boost bar."

Everyone laughed, and as they turned to leave, Vanessa's upper-class accent rang around the room once more.

"Hold on one minute, big boy. The last time we met, I gave you my card and asked you to call me sometime. I'm very disappointed that you haven't."

Gardener blushed again.

Chapter Twenty-four

Frankie had woken with a raging thirst, but that was nothing new. He was lucky he woke up at all most mornings, considering all the shit he shovelled down his throat.

He rolled out of bed and spent the next minute or so trying to find his woolly hat, before realizing it was still on his head. And he was still dressed. Going to bed fully dressed was nothing new for Frankie, he did that most nights; either because he'd passed out in a drunken stupor, or because he was simply too idle to remove his clothes, the latter reason being the most common, seeing as the shower in the caravan wasn't working – and hadn't been for some time. Who needed water anyway?

Frankie rummaged through his cupboards in an effort to find something edible. The first thing he came across was a bottle whose contents were light green in colour. His face changed expressions a dozen times as he squinted at the label. He couldn't read it. He chose the pot-luck option, pulled the top off and launched it down his throat.

He stopped quickly. Baulking, he stepped backwards, as if he'd been hit by a mechanical digger. The only reason he didn't spit it out was because he was too tight to part with anything. He scrambled around for a pair of glasses that he'd found in a skip at Specsavers. Once on, he scanned the label.

"Fucking cabbage juice," said Frankie. "Who drinks that shit?"

He held the bottle closer, sniffed at the liquid and had to pull his head back. He glanced at the label again.

"Oh well, waste not, want not."

Despite the fact that it didn't taste all that good, he continued drinking anyway.

Frankie had no idea of the time. He didn't possess a watch, so he reached over and switched on the radio, which was tuned to some sort of classic seventies channel. They were currently playing *Far, Far Away* by Slade, one of his favourite glam rock bands.

Frankie wobbled his girth a little before returning to the cupboard to see what crap he had salvaged from the supermarket skips the previous evening. He usually spent two or three nights a week at the shops, mostly as they were shutting, or afterwards. Paying a visit at closing time served two purposes; if he had to pay for something it was bound to be cheap. Alternatively, there was always plenty *in* the skip – still packaged.

Problem with last night was, it had been dark and he didn't have his glasses, so he had no idea what he was forcing into the carrier bags. The contents of his cupboard revealed sandwiches, buns, a variety of tinned goods, and a number of pies and pasties.

Grabbing one of the latter, Frankie noticed it was a chicken tikka slice. That would go down nicely for breakfast, along with the last of the cabbage juice. Once he'd finished that, he supposed he ought to spend some time outside the caravan. One fart after that concoction and he would blow the roof off. Frankie found that funny and tried to picture it.

He shuffled his way to the door and opened it, choosing to sit on the step outside. The sky was blue and the sun was facing him. A huge pile of cars in front of the van meant he couldn't be seen, but that wouldn't stop Mitchell finding him if Frankie was needed for a collection.

He tried to recollect the events of yesterday but aside from arriving at the pub and consuming large amounts of food and drink, he couldn't remember a great deal more. Apart from the fact that he'd had a scorching win on the horses. He suddenly remembered Mitchell sending him on an errand, which had taken him out of town. He'd sought out four bookmakers. Fools didn't know him. Placing bets on four different horses netted him something in the region of two thousand pounds.

Pasty and drink finished, Frankie suddenly jumped up and stepped back into the caravan. What the hell had he done with the money? He hoped he hadn't left it in the van he'd been driving. If Mitchell found it, Frankie might not see it again.

Running into the caravan was never a good idea, not with the stuff he had lying around. He remembered doing that once before, in bare feet, where he ended up with a mousetrap on each big toe. Frankie had fallen onto his bed, screaming in pain; the shaking in the van resembling a minor earthquake.

As expected, he did run into something. God only knew what, but it was heavy. Didn't matter to Frankie, he still had his rigger boots on. As that thought dawned on him, he realized he must have slept in those as well. He dived toward the bed and lifted the mattress but there was nothing there. He lifted the pillow – no money there either.

"Oh, fuck." Frankie panicked.

The song on the radio changed to *Ride A White Swan* by T-Rex, which momentarily took his mind off the money.

"Get in," shouted Frankie, rocking his girth in all directions. He stayed that way until *Money For Nothing* by Dire Straits diverted his attention.

He turned. The van had a total of three cupboards and having searched each one, he could not find the money in any of those. Within minutes his home resembled the scene of a break-in. He scurried to the toilet, but it wasn't to be found there either.

On the verge of hysteria, he left the bathroom and headed in the direction of the front door. He stumbled against a wall, lost his balance and fell toward the doorframe but managed to save himself with one hand. Whilst trying to think, he placed his left hand in the pocket of his body warmer and felt the crisp paper notes.

Dragging the money out of his pocket he breathed a sigh of relief. That made him think a little more clearly and he remembered dividing the money up. The remainder was underneath his woolly hat; couldn't be too careful. No one searched your hat when they were robbing you.

Once he had it all together, he decided to pay a visit to the Morris Minor on bricks.

As he walked over to the car, he thought back to the scene of the van fire. Police and firemen all over it like a rash. Although he'd tried to keep his distance, Frankie was a nosey bastard and needed to know everything that was going on, so he had meandered as close as he could to hear what people were saying.

Frankie had completely shit himself when he overheard someone say that there was a body in the back of the van.

A body, *in* the van?

At that point, Frankie's knees went weak, his stomach lurched and he broke out into a sweat – possibly the first of the year. If he'd had the strength he would have run back to the yard, to the caravan, and locked the door, where it was very unlikely he would ever venture out again.

There wasn't supposed to have been anyone in the bastard thing. His instructions had been quite simple: turn up very early and set fire to it. Destroy any or all evidence. He'd been paid well for that little job.

Then the police had approached him and started asking questions. How much did he know? Had he seen anyone? Where did he live? Fuck that last one for a lark.

No one knew anything about Frankie, and that was the way he liked it. He did not claim benefits and he was not registered with a doctor or with any other authority on the planet – which meant, of course, that he didn't have a driving licence, but if Mitchell was willing to take the risk, so was Frankie. He didn't need a doctor. Frankie was as fit as a flea, which he put down to not being too clean. When he was a kid, he wouldn't bother washing his hands all that often, and if what he was eating fell on the floor he'd simply pick it up and carry on.

As far as Frankie was concerned, bring on Covid. He doubted very much he would catch it, but if he did, he'd show it who was boss. Derek Mitchell reckoned that whatever Frankie had would kill Covid stone dead anyway.

Frankie thought about the body in the van again. He had no idea who the hell it could be, and all attempts to speak to Davey Challenger post-fire – to find out who the fuck he'd put in there – had failed. He'd tried calling him several times; pointless sending texts, because Frankie couldn't read. Every call he had made to Challenger's phone had remained unanswered. The phone was switched off. He hadn't left any messages. Frankie wasn't daft; you leave a message, and they will find you.

He'd asked around but no one had seen Challenger recently. He hadn't been drinking in any of the usual pubs. Still, thought Frankie, shouldn't panic too much, he could be lying low.

But even if he was, who the fuck had been burned to death in the van fire? That had not been part of the deal. The body in the van left Frankie in a bit of a fix. It wouldn't be the first time. It might be the last if it all went tits up.

Furtively glancing around, Frankie opened the boot lid of the Minor 1000 and pulled a wooden box toward him, which was becoming heavier. He lifted the lid, positively drooling at the sight of all the money. He had no idea how much was in there, but it had to run into the tens of thousands. He wasn't really worried because only *he* knew it was there, and he checked it every day.

He placed yesterday's winnings inside the box, keeping back about three hundred pounds. There were a few good race meetings today and he wanted a bet. Frankie thought that he might also treat himself to an afternoon in the pub. Order the biggest fucking steak they had, wash it down with gallons of beer, and then crawl back to the van to sleep it off.

As he replaced the lid on the box and shut the boot of the car, he glanced around again. He would check all the other boxes of money before attempting to slink past the portacabin, hoping Mitchell wouldn't see, and give him a shitload of work.

As he stepped forward, his mind raced back to the van fire.

Frankie had set fire to the van; that much he knew. If whoever was on the inside had been alive, and the fuzz found out and managed to trace it back to him, he would be done for murder.

Yes, he was a bit of a lad. He'd torched the van – under instruction. He'd torched quite a few actually. He'd done a bit of thieving in his time. He'd broken the law on countless occasions, all petty shit. But he was not a murderer! He had never killed anyone – that much he did know.

The more Frankie thought about it, the more his thoughts wandered to the only person who could possibly have done it: Derrick Mitchell.

Had Mitchell found out about everything? In particular, had he found out that the third man in the post office robbery was Challenger? And if so, was it Challenger's body in the van? That would be one reason why Frankie had not been able to raise Challenger. He'd have a right fucking job now, thought Frankie, laughing – Challenger becoming the new Lazarus.

Mind you, if any of this was true, Frankie was in very serious trouble.

Mitchell was a dangerous man, and if he found out about Frankie's dirty double-dealing, Frankie would end up the same way as the man in the van – no doubt about that.

What should he do?

Another minute of hard thinking, which was enough exercise for one day, left Frankie believing there was only one course of action: anonymously tell the police before Mitchell decided to deal with *him*.

Chapter Twenty-five

Reilly brought the pool car to a halt and killed the engine. Turning to his partner, he said, "It's a different ball game now."

"You're right, Sean," said Gardener. "On the one hand it's made things easier, but on the other…"

"Life goes back to normal for us," said Reilly. "With a shedload of puzzles to work through."

"Nothing new, is it?" said Gardener. "It gives us a focus, and at least we have been heading in the right direction."

"Might also focus this lady's mind when we tell her," said Reilly, glancing at Grace Challenger's front door.

She had obviously seen them because the door was open. Her attire was a figure-hugging red dress that finished a little below the knee, which was the same colour as her hair.

Gardener left the car. He entered the property and immediately removed his shoes. His partner did the same, and they followed Grace through to the kitchen.

"You're just in time, officers. I've just made a fresh drink." She turned, almost begging. "I do hope you have some news for me; please say you've found him."

Gardener figured the conversation might be tougher than he had expected.

"Would you like to take a seat, Mrs Challenger?"

She glanced around, as if sensing bad news, perhaps wondering if it was possible that there might actually be another Mrs Challenger in the room. She did as he asked.

As Gardener took his seat, he noticed the kitchen was busy, as per usual. There were two small plastic trays with freshly picked vegetables, including carrots, green beans, onions and parsnips.

"I've collected too many," said Grace, "as usual. One would think I was feeding an army. Perhaps you can help me out and take a few."

Reilly came to the table with the teas. He took his seat.

"I've not heard anything from my husband but if he comes home, I would like to be prepared. I don't want him going hungry." She stopped talking, staring at Gardener. "You've found him, haven't you?"

"Yes," said Gardener, removing his hat and placing it on the table.

"It's not good, is it?"

"I'm afraid not."

Her eyes immediately watered, and her expression paled. She reached for a tissue.

"Was it *his* body in the van fire?"

"We had it confirmed this morning, Mrs Challenger."

Further tears flowed. She snivelled and blew her nose into the tissue.

"I had really hoped you wouldn't tell me that. Did he suffer? I suppose he must have done. No one burns alive without suff…"

She couldn't finish the sentence, glancing away.

"Would you like us to call someone?" asked Gardener. "Your parents, or another member of the family?"

"We can also call a family liaison officer," said Reilly. "Get her to come and sit with you, Grace, love."

She shook her head. "Excuse me, please." Grace left the table and headed for the bathroom.

Both men waited quietly until she returned. During her time in the bathroom she had washed her face, which had removed most of her make-up. Gardener thought she was actually prettier without it.

"I'm so sorry, detectives."

"You've no need to apologise, Mrs Challenger," said Gardener. "News like that doesn't come easy. We are here to help, so please lean on the force and the professionals if you feel you need to."

She nodded. "Thank you. Can I ask again, did he suffer?"

"It appears not."

"What do you mean? He was burned to death. He must have felt something."

"Grace, love," said Reilly. "We've just come from the pathologist. It is a little bit more complicated."

"How complicated?" asked Grace.

"What my partner is trying to say, Mrs Challenger," said Gardener, "is that we have evidence that suggests your husband was dead before the fire started."

"Before?" said Grace, her voice an octave higher. "You mean someone killed him? What did they do to him?"

"There was a poison present in his system."

Gardener went on to explain, very briefly, what Fitz had told them.

"Aconitine?" she said. "Oh my God, that's awful stuff."

"Do you know much about it?" asked Reilly.

"Only what I've read," said Grace. "I know that it's plant-based, but then most poisons are. Who poisoned him? How did they do it?"

"We are investigating, Mrs Challenger," said Gardener. "But we don't have any answers as yet."

Grace started to tear up again. "This is awful. Who would do something like that? That's really specialized stuff. Where would you even get something like that?"

"That's what we have to find out, Grace, love," said Reilly.

"Why would anyone want to murder my husband? He was only a postman, for God's sake. He didn't work for the CIA."

"We have discovered some other information, which suggests a possible reason for what's happened," said Gardener.

Grace raised her head to meet their eyes. "What?"

"Going back to the post office robberies," said Gardener. "On the day of the fourth robbery here in Bursley Bridge, he was not at work."

"He wasn't!" said Grace. "That doesn't mean he had anything to do with it."

"I'm afraid that's not the case," said Gardener.

"We also discovered that instead of there being two people involved in the post office robbery," said Reilly, "a third member appeared on the scene, with a gun. One of the girls who works there believes that it was your husband. She recognised his voice, and his eyes."

"I can't believe what you're telling me, officers. Why would he want to rob a post office? He worked for them. Was he involved in the other robberies in the area?"

"Not from what we can ascertain," said Gardener. "On the day of the first, he was with you in York, and for the other two robberies, he *was* at work."

"I just can't believe he would do something like that," said Grace. "Why? It's not as if we don't have money, or a nice place to live, or plenty of food. We don't go short of anything. Are you absolutely sure it was him?"

"Everything points to it, Mrs Challenger. We also have his prints on the gun and in the van."

"Oh, dear," said Grace, reaching for another tissue.

"Going back to the day of the robbery here in the town, last Friday," said Gardener. "Can you describe what you know of his day for me?"

"I'm not sure I follow you," said Grace. "Describe his day?"

"As far as you know, did he stick to his normal routine?"

Grace appeared to think about the question. "As far as I can remember, yes. He left on time, and in uniform."

"What time was that?"

"Somewhere around six," replied Grace.

"And you were up?" asked Reilly.

"I'm always up, officer. I like to see that he has a good breakfast, and I pack him a little something up for the day."

Gardener found her dedication endearing.

"He returned home a little later than usual, around five o'clock, still in uniform. He showered. We ate together, and then he went out," said Grace, tearing up again.

Gardener allowed her a minute or two to compose herself, after which she apologised again.

"The thing is, Mrs Challenger," said Gardener, "because it is now a murder investigation, we really do need to change the way we do things."

"What do you mean?"

"We have to look much deeper into everyone's lives. The last time we were here we asked about computers and you mentioned that your husband used his own laptop and iPad."

"Most of the time, yes."

"Do you have a home computer, and did he use it at all?"

"Yes," said Grace. "On occasions."

"Can we take your computer, please? We will also need to take your phone, and have you found his phone yet?"

"No," said Grace. "If he didn't have it with him, I have no idea where it could be. I have searched the house for it, but it's not in here."

Gardener nodded. He really would have liked her husband's phone.

"With your permission, we would also like to search the house."

"I didn't think you needed my permission, officer," said Grace. "But I do appreciate you asking. May I ask one thing?"

"By all means," replied Gardener.

"All I ask is that you leave the place as you find it."

"Of course," said Gardener, figuring that's what she was going to say.

"Am I a suspect?" asked Grace.

"Please don't take this the wrong way, Mrs Challenger, but at the moment, we have to treat everyone as a suspect."

Her eyes widened. "Am I under arrest?"

"No," said Gardener, "just helping us with our inquiries."

"Do I need a solicitor?"

"Only if you *think* you need one, Grace, love," said Reilly. "If you haven't done anything wrong, you won't."

"I can assure you, officers," said Grace, "I had nothing whatsoever to do with those robberies. But I sincerely hope that you find out who has, because I'd like to know what my husband was mixed up in."

Grace rose from the table.

"I'll get the items you requested, and if you can let me know when you want to search the house, I'll make sure everything is ready for you."

Thirty minutes later, with everything in place, Gardener and Reilly left Grace Challenger's property as the SOCOs were pulling in with their van. Following a quick word, Gardener said he had to be elsewhere but would call back before they left.

"What do you think?" asked Reilly.

"On the whole, I think she took it quite well," said Gardener. "But I've just had another thought."

"About what?" asked Reilly.

"Aconitine," said Gardener. "Both Fitz and Vanessa Chambers suggested it was a specialised product. You have to know what you're doing when handling it. And while we were talking to Grace, she said exactly the same thing."

"What are you thinking?"

"That administering aconitine would take a skilled person."

"Like a nurse, you mean?" suggested Reilly.

"It had crossed my mind," said Gardener.

"But surely the nurse you're thinking of has an alibi," said Reilly. "Monica Rushby was working."

"That's what worries me," said Gardener.

He grabbed his mobile and called Bob Anderson, explaining what Fitz had told them. He then asked that they call on Monica Rushby. Now that it was a murder investigation, he wanted her computer and her phone, and he was going to organise a search of her house as well.

Chapter Twenty-six

The following morning, Grace was shown into the offices of Powell and Potter in Bursley Bridge. They had been the family solicitors for as long as anyone could remember. As the business had grown considerably over the years, so had Norman Powell, whose girth was now probably three times what it had been in the early years. He'd somehow managed to force his corpulent frame into a small seat behind a small desk in a small office, or perhaps it simply appeared that way.

As Grace took a seat, the solicitor grunted whilst still sifting through his paperwork, scrawling a signature every now and again. The office had a Victorian fireplace with a fully loaded fire, which was currently spitting and crackling away. Most of the furniture was wooden, with a number of glass cabinets overstuffed with books and files, a coffee table and two armchairs, a stained mirror above the fireplace, and a rug that was probably older than Powell.

"I shan't keep you, Mrs Challenger," he said, peering through a pair of pince-nez perched precariously on the end of his nose.

His grey thatch was thick and showed no signs of abating, despite his advancing years. His head was large and his features were all quite small and rodent-like, apart from his jowls.

Powell, who was wearing a grey suit with a white shirt, blue tie, and a grey waistcoat as always, finished signing his papers, shuffled them all together and placed them in a folder. At that point, his secretary stepped into the office with tea, and an assortment of digestives on a large silver tray – at least half a packet. She smiled at Grace, took the paperwork and left the office.

Powell clasped his hands together and placed them under his chins.

"Thank you for calling me, and for coming in. I was in fact about to call you."

"Me?" said Grace. "Whatever for?"

"Shall we have some tea, Mrs Challenger?" said Powell, glancing at the grandfather clock in the corner that Grace had somehow failed to notice. "I do so enjoy my elevenses. I can't quite imagine getting through the day without it."

Whether Grace had wanted it or not, the tea had been poured and a saucer of digestives was placed in front of her.

Powell immediately devoured at least half a dozen of the biscuits – four of which had been dunked in the tea – before wiping his mouth with a napkin.

"As I said, I was about to call you before you called me."

"What about?" asked Grace, the feeling in the pit of her stomach growing more intense.

"Well," said Powell, "this unfortunate business of a body in a van fire."

"Do you know about that?"

"I do now," replied Powell. "It does help to keep one's finger on the pulse." He quickly ate another three digestives before continuing. "There is a police website that lists… well, shall we say the unsavoury things that happen in their day-to-day engagements. And although they put out press releases, appealing for witnesses to crimes, they usually post it on their site immediately, which can of course produce much quicker results."

Grace's stomach turned. "And the van fire is on their site?"

"Yes," said Powell.

"And have they mentioned my husband?"

"Yes," said Powell.

"And they're appealing for witnesses to help find out who did it?"

"Yes," said Powell, unable, it appeared, to say anything else.

"You'd have thought they'd have told me," she said.

"They didn't?"

"No."

"I assume that's what you wanted to talk to me about," said Powell.

"In a fashion," replied Grace.

"You mean there is something else?"

"There certainly is," replied Grace. "Is that what you wanted to talk to me about, the body in the van fire?"

"In a fashion," repeated Powell, who appeared to grow more uncomfortable as the conversation progressed.

"Okay," said Grace. "Would you like to start?"

"Perhaps you could, my dear," said Powell. "Your body language suggests to me that there is something concerning you that I'm not yet aware of."

Grace was thinking the same about Powell, which really was putting her off. After some thought, she explained that the police had called to see her, searched her house and then removed most of her electronic devices.

"Really?" said Powell. "So the police have evidence that your husband was involved in the robberies?"

"Only the fourth," said Grace.

"And you knew nothing about this?"

"No. I couldn't believe it when they told me. *My* husband, a man I have known for over twenty years appears to have been leading a double, or even a triple life, or more than that for all I know."

"And he gave nothing away?"

"No," said Grace. "And if he had, do you think I would have stood for it?"

Powell's bushy eyebrows inched further up his head. "Absolutely not, my dear."

"This is why I came to see you. They've taken all my devices, including my phone. What if they find something on me? What if my husband, who's been up to no good, has implicated me in some way? I'm going to need a solicitor."

"Quite," said Powell. "But they would have to *prove* it."

"Well that would depend on what they found," said Grace.

Powell shifted uncomfortably, causing his chair to creak and his desk to slide.

"They'd still have to prove it," he said. "But I *can* see your predicament."

"So would you represent me in court?"

Powell flinched. He obviously hadn't liked that question but recovered well.

"Of course we will, Mrs Challenger, but I must point out it's not my area of expertise. I personally deal with wills and other family matters, but we have another branch in York and I will put you in touch with a solicitor who is more than capable of representing you."

Grace sighed. "That's certainly a weight off my mind. You have been our family's solicitor for that many years, we're almost friends."

"Thank you," said Powell. "We like to think of ourselves that way. Talking of family, do yours know?"

"They know about the van fire."

"But not the other stuff?"

"No," said Grace, "I think I'd die of shame."

"Don't you think they have a right to know?"

"Not yet," she said. "You won't tell them, will you?"

Powell shook his head. "No. But they're going to find out, once this hits the newspapers, and it will."

"Anyway, I'm innocent. I had absolutely nothing to do with those robberies. Whatever he was up to, he was doing so without my consent or my knowledge."

"Very pleased to hear it," said Powell, glancing at the clock.

"Now," said Grace, "what was it you wanted to talk to me about?"

"Pardon?" said Powell.

"You said you were going to call me before I called you; about what?"

Powell shifted uncomfortably again, loosened his tie, fished a handkerchief out of his top pocket and dabbed at his brow, and then checked his cup to see how much tea was left.

"It's another delicate matter, Mrs Challenger," he said, reaching into a drawer in his desk, removing a folder.

"How delicate?" asked Grace. "It can't be any worse than the problems I already have."

"I wouldn't bank on that," said Powell, almost under his breath, removing paperwork from the folder.

"Sorry?" said Grace.

"Just coming to that," said Powell.

He read through the papers, as if he hadn't already, and arranged them on the desk in front of him.

"Once I heard the news, and you had telephoned, I took the liberty of examining your husband's will."

"Oh, yes, of course," said Grace. "I hadn't really given that any thought. I suppose I didn't want to. Even though we hadn't been getting along too well…" Her eyes watered and she made a grab for a tissue in her bag. Dabbing them, she said, "I would still rather he was here. And trust me, if he was, he would certainly get a piece of my mind."

"I don't doubt that, Mrs Challenger," said Powell. "And after I tell you what I know, I suspect an even bigger slice would be on offer."

"Why?" questioned Grace, feeling sick.

"Look, Mrs Challenger, as his wife you are legally entitled to half of everything, if not all of it, and you would be quite within your rights to contest the will."

"Contest it?" said Grace, taken aback. "Why would I contest it?"

Powell clasped his hands together and leaned further forward, lowering his voice, as if somehow the whole world was a party to his next statement.

"I'm afraid your husband changed his will some time back."

"Changed it?"

"Yes, I'm afraid so."

"And?"

"I have to tell you that you are not the main beneficiary."

Grace almost stopped breathing. Her chest tightened, and she struggled to remain as calm as possible.

"Not the main beneficiary?" she questioned. "Who is?"

"That, I can't tell you, Mrs Challenger."

Chapter Twenty-seven

"Monica?"

Monica jumped at the sound of her name. She glanced upwards and saw Grace, a relatively new friend, someone she had met only two or three months back.

"Are you okay, Monica, love? You look terrible."

Monica shook her head and cried into her tissue. "Not really."

"Oh, dear, are you having one of those days?"

"I wish it was only one day, and not several," replied Monica, between sobs.

She'd been in the café in Bursley Bridge for twenty minutes or more and had yet to order. The staff had also asked if she was okay and she'd told them she was, bar for a touch of upsetting news, but she promised she'd order something eventually, and so they left her alone.

The café was rustic, with plenty of wood and glass, and fabric seating, some of which were big, antiquated armchairs set around small coffee tables. The real bonus was they baked cakes like no one on Earth, which was why trade was always brisk.

"You know what you need," said Grace, leaning toward Monica, "and I'm not taking no for an answer."

"I do," said Monica. "But I doubt I could find it here."

By that time, Grace was already halfway to the counter. When she returned almost five minutes later, she had a tray containing tea, one of their famous brick-sized vanilla slices, and some kind of fruit compote.

"The world always looks better through a vanilla slice."

Under normal circumstances, Monica couldn't agree more. "Why aren't you having one, then?"

"Got to watch my figure," said Grace.

Monica doubted that – it was almost hourglass. Grace was pretty flawless even though she had no make-up on today, or very little that Monica could detect. She was dressed in a pale lemon two-piece trouser suit, with a designer bag and no doubt designer shoes.

"Besides, you seem to need one more than me," said Grace.

"Who do you have to watch your figure for?" asked Monica. "You're single, no one to answer to…"

That was the point at which Monica could not complete the sentence. Her stomach flipped and the tears flowed. Though Monica was not married either, there had been the possibility on the horizon. In a cruel twist of fate she had now lost the only man she had ever really felt something for, despite knowing little about him. Strangely enough, she hadn't felt she needed to. It was as though she had known him all her life.

"What's wrong, Monica, love?" asked Grace.

Monica realized Grace was another of those people she knew very little about but felt she had a real soulmate by her side. All that Monica really knew was that Grace lived locally, kept her own company and, by all accounts had a lovely house with a garden full of herbs and vegetables that she grew herself.

"He's gone," said Monica.

"Who has?" asked Grace, sipping her herbal tea.

Monica plucked up the courage to tell Grace what had happened. She would have to eventually tell someone that the police had been to the house, and about her boyfriend who had been missing presumed dead; and now *was* dead.

"Dead, how?" asked Grace, and then suddenly put her hand to her mouth. "You don't mean he was the man in that awful van fire, do you?"

Monica nodded, crying into a fresh tissue, her drink and pastry untouched.

"Oh, Monica, that must be awful," said Grace. "And then the police turning up and taking all your devices. They can't honestly think you're involved, surely."

"I don't think so," said Monica.

"But they must suspect something, otherwise they wouldn't take all your devices."

Monica almost shrieked, her stomach turning inside out.

"Oh, God, you don't think so, do you? They can't think I had anything to do with his murder. I loved the man. I wouldn't kill him."

"Don't worry, Monica. I didn't mean anything, I'm sure it's just routine. But why would they take your phone and your computer? Has *he* been up to something dodgy, is that why he ended up in the van?"

Monica nodded, amazed at how Grace always seemed to have the ability to guess what you were thinking before you said it.

She told Grace what little she knew about the robberies and Davey's involvement.

"What, all of them?" Grace asked.

"Probably," said Monica.

"That's awful, Monica," said Grace. "If he was involved in all of that stuff he must have been mixed up with some pretty dodgy people. No wonder that happened."

"How would I know. I was working on all of the dates that the robberies were committed."

Monica slammed her palm on the table, startling a couple nearby.

"That's all I bloody well do, work. And to think, all I ever wanted was to be a nurse, and look where it's got me: bloody nowhere; early forties, on the shelf and no future."

Grace reached out and touched Monica's hand. "Now, now, it's not as bad as all that. You need to concentrate on all the positives."

"What are they?"

"You're young, have your own house, a good steady job. You'll always have a job being a nurse. The NHS is crying out for nurses. You concentrate on why you wanted to become a nurse, saving all those lives."

"I couldn't save Davey's, could I?"

Grace appeared to flinch at that statement.

"No, love, you couldn't, but then you didn't know. I'm sure if you had, you'd have done everything possible."

Grace pulled back, her mood switching almost at the flick of a switch.

"I couldn't do your job, really, I couldn't. What made *you* want to?"

Monica thought about that, unsure of whether or not she was in the mood to relate what had happened all those years ago.

"It's a long story."

"We're not going anywhere," said Grace. "Tell me. It'll make you feel better."

Monica smiled, wondering if that was possible.

She relived the incident very clearly, witnessing an accident as a child on Boar Lane in Leeds. She was eight years old and was having a girls' day out with her mother.

A young boy, following an argument with his mother, threw a tantrum and, without paying attention to what he was doing, ran into the road. A truck driver, his load bearing down upon the boy, had applied his brakes only to find they did not work. He swerved in order to avoid hitting him, and crashed into a bus full of passengers instead. Although no one was killed, almost everyone at the scene was either shaken or injured, one or two of them more seriously.

Monica watched on as ambulance men battled on. Eventually, her and her mother helped, by kneeling and talking to some of the injured whilst the medics saw to them. A number of shopkeepers on the scene quickly prepared tea and coffee and Monica handed those out. She found that helping people was something she enjoyed. She felt she was good at it.

Monica finished her story and finally sipped her tea.

"Has that made you feel better?" asked Grace.

"Strangely enough, a little."

After a lapsed silence, Monica said, "I got a call about an hour ago, from a solicitor."

"A solicitor," repeated Grace. "What about?"

"Apparently," said Monica, "Davey has left everything to me in his will."

Chapter Twenty-eight

Gardener faced the team. The incident room was full.

"We've had a busy couple of days, and this is the first chance I've had to share some important information with you since we saw Fitz yesterday."

Gardener went on to confirm that the body in the van was Challenger, and to inform them of what it was that had killed him.

"This is how I see it," said Gardener. "We can't pin down Challenger's movements exactly on the day leading up to his death. The last anyone saw of him was Grace, at seven-thirty on the Friday night. After he left the house he was not seen again. He did not go and see Monica Rushby and he certainly didn't go to the pub. The only conclusion I can come to is, he met with the other robbers and something went wrong. He was killed, dumped in the van and more than likely driven to the spot where the vehicle was torched."

"He was definitely dead before the fire, then?" asked Anderson. "At least that was something."

"It doesn't sit right with me," said Rawson. "There's something wrong with this scenario. Gangland thieves just don't operate like this. Wouldn't they have put a gun to his head and have done with it?"

"That's more likely," said Benson.

"Okay," said Gardener. "There is no doubt that Davey Challenger is our man, but we need to find out the rest. What were his movements on the day? Hopefully, we can find someone who did actually see and speak to him during the times we can't place him anywhere."

Gardener was keen to find out about the seizure of the home computers and phones from Monica Rushby and Grace Challenger.

"Do they reveal anything?"

"No," said Gates.

"Nothing?" asked Gardener.

"Nothing on either," said Longstaff. "There was absolutely nothing on either home computer, or on the phones that gave us a clue to what Challenger was up to."

"Apart from an extramarital affair," said Gates. "There was some pretty steamy stuff between Challenger and Monica. We have found mention of them wanting to move to the Algarve but nothing concrete had actually been done about that."

Gardener shook his head. "I can't believe there isn't some compromising information on there."

"It suggests one thing," said Cragg.

"Go on," said Gardener.

"That when both women claimed to know nothing about the robbery, or the murder, they might have been telling the truth."

"Possibly," said Gardener. "But we have a line of inquiry that I'll come back to, which possibly puts one of them in the frame."

"Interesting," said Rawson. "I hope it's Grace, I'd definitely like another look at her."

"Christ!" said Reilly. "There's no stopping the man."

"Only saying," said Rawson, sheepishly.

"Well, when we get to the end of this," said Gardener, "if she's innocent then maybe you can go and pay her another visit."

"Good luck with that one," said Reilly. "She's well out of your league, mister."

Before Rawson could reply, Gardener took the reins again.

"Okay, there is now a need to dig deeper. I'd like to know why he has alibis for the first three."

"Doesn't mean he wasn't involved," said Cragg.

"I agree," replied Gardener, "but why change pattern?"

"Especially as it seems to have got him killed," added Reilly.

"It's a pretty safe bet that he *was* involved in the others," said Gardener. "Maybe he was a sleeping partner, and he wasn't happy with the share-out. Perhaps he was getting less because he wasn't taking any risks."

"He was definitely in the right place to collect information," said Reilly. "Being a postman gave him the best opportunity to stake the places out and figure out the best days to attack. There's no end to what he could bring to the table."

"Which is probably the reason they had been so successful," said Cragg.

"Can someone talk to his employer again?" asked Gardener. "Find out his general routine, his routes, and in particular, where he was on the days of the robberies."

"Good idea," said Cragg. "If he was on those routes on the right days, maybe he *was* involved. He could have been hanging around inconspicuously, just in the right place to oversee everything went smoothly."

"We could do to go through all the witness statements again," said Reilly. "See if there is a mention of a post office van anywhere in sight on the days of the robberies."

"Good point, Sean," said Gardener. "That's a job for someone. We definitely need to know who else was involved in these robberies."

"If they weren't local," said Edwards, "we're going to have our work cut out."

Gardener shook his head. "Not so sure anymore, Patrick. I don't buy into an out-of-town gang operating on this patch. I honestly think it is someone local, and until now they have no track record." He turned to Cragg. "Maurice, I know you've been through this once already, but can you involve the old boy's network, see if there is something going down that we haven't yet unearthed?"

Cragg nodded. "I can give it another go."

"Who has Challenger upset?" asked Gardener. "How did he become involved in all of this? In other words, how has he gone from postman, to post office robber?"

"Still no word on his phone?" asked Reilly.

Each of them shook their heads.

"That's really our biggest problem," said Gardener. "I think we can safely say that the electronic equipment he used was the stuff that was destroyed in the van fire, so we're bang out of luck with that."

"Maybe," said Gates, "but we do have his phone number from Grace and Monica's phone."

"Yes," said Longstaff. "We have tried calling but it's still switched off. So we've been in touch with his provider and asked them for a list of all his calls and texts for the last six months."

"Excellent," said Gardener. "That's a breakthrough, one that might help us pin down more people who can provide more information. Well done, ladies."

Gardener made notes on the whiteboard and then continued.

"Another problem we have at the moment is that there are really only two people in the frame, both of which look very unlikely to be involved with either the robberies or the death, but they can't be ruled out."

"Grace and Monica?" asked Anderson.

Gardener nodded. "Both have alibis but only Monica's is watertight. She was working on the night of every robbery. And given what you've said about her computer and phone history, I simply can't see how she can be involved."

"Or Grace," suggested Gates. "Her phone and computer are also clean."

"But we now have a medical element in the investigation, which gives Monica a possible connection," said Gardener. "Aconitine might be derived from something else at the hospital. So I think we need someone checking out that side of things. Hospitals, doctor's surgeries, pharmacies; are their records of aconitine correct? Has everything been signed out correctly? Is there anything missing that can't be accounted for?"

Gardener turned to the whiteboards adding further notes before returning his attention to his team.

"Does anyone have anything else? What about the accelerant used on the van?"

"We're still waiting for the CCTV from Birmingham, sir," said Benson.

"We know the day, and roughly the time," said Edwards. "So we're calling just about every hour. I don't think they think it's as important as we do."

"They never have much time to themselves," said Benson. "Apparently they have thousands of people a day going through the place."

"They soon won't have," said Gardener, "with rising fuel prices. But keep at it. The faster we get that, the quicker we might be able to tie this up. Tell them we want the information by close of play today or they'll have me to deal with."

He turned to Gates and Longstaff. "Now that we have a registration, what about CCTV on the burnt-out van?"

"Nothing much," said Gates.

"Only spotted once," added Longstaff, "shortly after it was bought, driving through the town."

"But it was only fleeting," said Gates. "It wasn't possible to plot where it went as no further CCTV picked it up."

"Okay," said Gardener. "Something else to keep going with. We only need one small break."

He turned to Benson and Edwards. "Anything on photos of where the vans in the robberies were bought? Did anyone manage to produce a photo from CCTV?"

"We have one, sir." Benson passed it to Gardener, who passed it to Cragg, who shook his head.

"Can't say I recognise him," he said.

"Okay," said Gardener.

Cragg passed it back and the SIO attached it to the whiteboard.

At that point, the door opened and Tom Wilkinson popped his head through.

"I'm so sorry, I seem to have missed everything."

Gardener greeted him. "Not to worry. Sean and I can take you through what we've discovered."

"I'm so sorry," he said again. "I got caught at one of the cafés we have here. Can't seem to help myself. Every day, I spot a cake that I just have to try."

"Can't fault you there, Tom, old son," said Reilly. "So maybe you'll have to let me know the name of that there café and I can be paying a visit, so I can."

Gardener turned, raised his hand to his head. "Oh, Jesus, here we go."

"I will," said Wilkinson. "But on this occasion, my bad little habit has paid us a real dividend."

"Go on," said Gardener, Wilkinson having grabbed his full attention.

"Well, I was sitting there minding my own business, making notes, when I heard a familiar voice. I stopped, looked up, and who should I see engaged in conversation together but Grace Challenger and Monica Rushby?"

Chapter Twenty-nine

"I'm pleased you've called so quickly," said Grace. "I know how busy you must be."

Gates and Longstaff had taken a seat at the table, as their host had requested. So far, Gates had not mentioned why they had called to see her, but she had always been one for playing her cards close to her chest. If you gave someone the opportunity to speak, it was surprising what they would reveal.

Grace placed a tray on the table with tea and biscuits and took her seat.

"Please, help yourselves. I often think about the hours you people must work. I bet you never get the time for proper meals."

Longstaff glanced at Gates but said nothing.

"Where's that nice Detective Inspector with the hat?" asked Grace.

"The boss man," said Longstaff. "He'll be busy with something. He always is, never switches off."

"And his Irish friend." Grace smiled. "There's a man with an appetite."

"You're telling me," said Gates. Keen to steer the conversation in the right direction, she asked, "What can we help you with, Mrs Challenger? You called the station and said you'd discovered something of high importance."

Grace rose and left the table, crossed the kitchen to the plastic tray full of vegetables where she scooped something out. When she returned and sat down, she slid a mobile phone across.

"Whose is that?" asked Longstaff.

"My husband's," said Grace.

"Where did you find it?" asked Gates, without touching it.

"Hidden in the garage."

"Hidden?" questioned Longstaff. "How would you define, hidden?"

"I suppose that's the wrong word," replied Grace. "I didn't have to turn the place upside down for it, but it was on one of the shelves toward the back."

"Did you find anything else?" asked Gates, checking to see if the phone was still switched off. It was.

"Such as?" asked Grace.

Cool customer, thought Gates. "Anything else that might help with the investigation?"

"I certainly didn't find any money," said Grace. "No, officers, there wasn't anything else. It was pretty much like any other garage in the country, full of clutter and no organization to it."

"Will you have any reason to go back in there?" asked Gates.

Longstaff was busy examining the phone and appeared not to be taking any notice of the questions.

"Only to park my car in there."

"Where is your car at the moment?"

"Being serviced by the local garage. They're very good, they always collect and deliver so it saves me going to any trouble. Why are you asking about my garage?"

"We would like to seal it off and have a look around the place ourselves."

Gates wondered why Grace's garage had not been checked by the SOCOs on their previous visit. That was something she would have to check.

"Have you switched the phone on?" asked Longstaff.

"I did, yes," said Grace, sheepishly, as if she felt she might have done something wrong.

"Did any messages come through at all?"

"No," replied Grace.

"Will you excuse me for a minute?" asked Longstaff. She left the room, returning quickly with a Faraday bag, immediately placing the phone inside and sealing it.

"Have you studied any of the messages that were already on the phone?" asked Gates.

"I did, yes."

"Is there anything that you think we need to know about?"

"I don't want to speak out of turn here," said Grace.

Gates wondered why she had said that. "Anything that you tell us, Mrs Challenger, will be dealt with in the strictest confidence."

"I'm not sure," said Grace. "You hear of such awful things."

"Mrs Challenger," said Longstaff, sternly. "If you know something that will help us with the investigation, either by leading us to the post office robberies, or the person who killed your husband, you have a moral duty of care to tell us."

"You obviously do know something," said Gates. "Please tell us, Mrs Challenger. We'll relay all of that information to DI Gardener and he will be the best judge of how to act."

Grace appeared to relax at the sound of Gardener's name. "I think I might know who is responsible for the robberies."

"Go on," said Gates.

Longstaff immediately produced a pad and pen.

"There are a couple of conversations with a name that I don't know," said Grace. "I have no idea how my husband knew this person, but it's obvious to me that he has somehow roped him into something beyond his control. Quite how, I have no idea."

Money is usually a good motivator, thought Gates.

"Who is it?" asked Longstaff.

"He's called Frankie. From what I've heard, I think *he's* responsible for the post office robberies."

Gates glanced at Longstaff.

"Is this person known to the police?" asked Grace, as if she had picked up on the expressions between Longstaff and herself.

"He has come up in the course of the investigation," said Gates.

"Then why haven't you arrested him?" demanded Grace. "You might have saved my husband's life."

Gates ignored the question. "What makes you think Frankie is responsible for the post office robberies?"

"Study the phone, officer. For some reason my husband recorded conversations between himself and Frankie. I think there is enough information to suggest what they were all up to. But from what I understand, it's my guess that my husband found out something he shouldn't have done. He did, after all, work for the post office; but then perhaps he was silenced for his trouble."

Gates thought Grace had stopped, but Grace went on, "Possibly blackmailed, and then silenced."

"Okay," said Gates. "We will study all the information very carefully and take the appropriate course of action. We certainly appreciate you bringing this to our attention."

"Does the appropriate course of action include protecting me?" asked Grace. "You know, a safe house and a new identity and all that palaver?"

"We will certainly consider your position in all of this," said Gates. "Why do you feel the need for such a high level of protection?"

"Why?" demanded Grace. "Because they're villains! That Frankie character and whoever else he was working with must have found out something they didn't like about Davey and taken care of him."

"There's a lot going on there, Mrs Challenger," said Gates. "We will need to substantiate it, but your protection will be uppermost in our minds."

"I should think it is," said Grace. "Having told you all this, I now fear for my own safety. I don't want to be left vulnerable with so many dangerous people out there. If my husband has double-crossed them in any way, they will come after me. What if he's hidden the money somewhere? They're going to be looking for their share and it won't take them long to find me. Who knows what they'll do – torture me, pull my fingernails out to make me talk. Oh, I couldn't bear that. I don't know anything. But they won't believe that, will they?"

Gates thought there was no stopping Grace now she was on that track. She was like an express train with faulty brakes. She had to somehow find a way to derail her but thankfully, Longstaff's interjection did that.

"There are other things to consider here, Mrs Challenger."

"Such as?" asked Grace.

"Well, your husband was poisoned for one thing, and the compound used on him was very specialized."

"Explaining the aconitine in his system is a real puzzle for us," said Gates. "In our experience, gangs are not really into specialized poison. They tend to employ the traditional method, a bullet to the brain."

"How do you know they *didn't* shoot him?" said Grace. "Maybe the poison was to throw you off the scent."

"We have the post-mortem results," said Longstaff. "Trust me, your husband was not shot."

The room descended into silence and before Gates could proceed with her next questions, Grace spoke again.

"I just might be able to shed some light on that, actually."

Once again, her statement was delivered in a sheepish way, as if she wasn't really bothered about telling everything she knew, but she simply wanted Gates and Longstaff to tease it out of her.

"The poison?" said Longstaff.

"I'm only putting two and two together and I might be making five."

"Let us be the judge, Mrs Challenger," said Gates.

"I know someone who works in that area who, shall we say, is not all she's cracked up to be."

"Monica Rushby, you mean?" said Longstaff.

She operated very much like Sean Reilly, if something had to be said, she said it, with no regard for the effects of lighting the blue touchpaper.

Grace's expression grew dark and thunderous as her features pinched.

"We wondered if you might mention her," said Gates. "Do you often meet in cafés?"

"How do you know about that?"

"We didn't find out from you, did we?" asked Longstaff.

"We used to," said Grace, relenting somewhat. "Until yesterday. I shall choose my friends more carefully in the future."

Gates, who had been taking a sip of tea, almost spat it across the table, the term having taken her completely by surprise.

Even Longstaff had stopped writing.

"She's your *friend*?" asked Gates, trying to work out how that was possible, knowing what they now knew. The implications raced around her head.

"Was," replied Grace, indignantly.

"And she isn't now, because?" asked Longstaff, obviously as keen as Gates to hear the explanation.

Grace suddenly produced a tissue and sobbed into it. When finished, she spluttered out, "I have just discovered that the brazen hussy was my husband's mistress. They have been carrying on behind my back. How stupid do you think that makes me look?"

"With all due respect," said Longstaff, "you told DI Gardener that you and your husband had not been getting along for some time. Did you not consider something like an affair might be the reason?"

Gates nearly squirmed at the directness of the approach.

"I had no idea why we hadn't been getting along," replied Grace. "Knowing what I know now, it could have been any number of reasons: the affair, the robberies, fearing for his life. Take your pick."

"Forgive me for asking," said Gates, "but you seem to be implying that Monica Rushby had something to do with your husband's death. Why would you say that?"

"I'm only pointing out what I know. She's the main beneficiary of his will. He has left her everything he had, which, in my book, gives her a motive, especially if she needs money. There was poison in his system. She's a nurse; who better to know about poisons?"

"Once again," said Gates, "forgive the question, but what exactly did your husband leave her in his will? Did he leave her a lot of money, or this house, or anything valuable that you had?"

"I've no idea," replied Grace, "because my solicitor won't tell me. But maybe she has the money from the robbery, or maybe my husband was involved in all of them and had been salting it away in a secret bank account for the pair of them to live on. I don't know. Maybe she has some connection to Frankie. All I know is that I am devastated by all of this, and at a time when you need your friends around you, I have just found out that one of the very few I have, isn't."

Chapter Thirty

After speaking to Gates and Longstaff, Gardener and Reilly had decided to pay another visit to Monica, which was something they had planned to do anyway but the SIO felt it more important now, after everything they had told him.

Having studied her phone and computer, Gardener had seen nothing whatsoever to link Monica to the robberies, and very little – other than the fact she was having a relationship with him – to link her to Davey's death. Although there was nothing on Monica's phone, if she was clever enough to have an involvement, she could well have disguised everything by using a second phone. That was something he would have to wait and see because they had only found Challenger's phone earlier in the day.

Despite Monica's cast-iron alibis, he couldn't ignore Grace's not so subtle accusations, or the other information she had brought to the table. As far as Grace was concerned however, her implication of Monica may simply be sour grapes, but not without reason after what she had learned of her husband's will.

Once again, everyone was seated in the kitchen, which to be honest was not as tidy as the last time they'd seen it, but Gardener was pleased to hear the radio, which meant Monica was still clinging to some kind of reality. She was actually dressed in a denim boilersuit that bore a number of different coloured paint stains, with her hair hanging limply on her shoulders.

It seemed to Gardener that she was taking Davey's death much harder than his wife, but, as Grace had intimated, she and her husband had not been conversing too well of late.

"What's happened?" said Monica. "Do you know any more about Davey, and who killed him and set the van on fire?"

"We are looking into it, Miss Rushby," said Gardener.

"Which probably means you don't." Her eyes glazed over and teared up. "I'm not blaming you, officer. God knows how hard your job must be. I certainly wouldn't like to have to do it."

"There are times when we don't, Monica, love," said Reilly. "But if we didn't, there would be a lot more bad guys out there."

"I don't doubt it," replied Monica, flatly. "So, how can I help you?"

"Do you know anyone by the name of Frankie?" asked Gardener.

"Who?" asked Monica. "Frankie, who the bloody hell is he?"

"You've not come across anyone of that name?" persisted Gardener.

Monica shook her head. "Well, I might have done at some point in my life, but not recently."

"The man we're talking about is a strange little character who helps run a scrapyard at the bottom of East Ings Lane," said Gardener.

"If you saw him, Monica, love, you'd never forget him," said Reilly. "He's the stuff of nightmares."

"No shortage of them at the moment," she replied. "I knew there was a scrapyard down there, but I've no idea who runs it. I've never had reason to go over there."

"What about Derrick Mitchell?"

Monica took a sip of tea and scrunched up her face. Gardener wasn't sure if it was the tea, or the fact that she was running that name through her head.

"No, sorry," she replied. "Does he help this Frankie character?"

"Not really," said Reilly. "It's Frankie who helps Mitchell."

"And what are they to do with me?"

"Nothing that we know of, Miss Rushby," said Gardener.

"But they must have something to do with Davey, otherwise you wouldn't ask."

"Frankie and Davey have been linked."

"Are they involved in the robberies?" she asked, taking her medication with another drink of tea.

"It's an avenue we're pursuing," said Gardener.

"Oh my God, did this Frankie kill Davey? Is he responsible for all the robberies and the murder, and setting the van on fire?"

"We don't know, Monica, love," said Reilly. "We're still trying to join the dots."

"But Davey is linked to them?"

"As my sergeant says, Miss Rushby, we're not sure about that yet. It is a complicated case and we really do have to check every lead given to us."

Monica nodded but said nothing. She took another sip of tea and then asked, "I assume I can't have my phone or my computer back just yet?"

Gardener shook his head. "I'm afraid not."

"It's okay. It's not as if I have a use for it."

"Are you off work at the moment?" asked Gardener.

"Yes, they've given me some leave. I was due some anyway, and this was as good a time as any. I doubt I could concentrate on anything."

Gardener decided to change subjects. "Do you know a lady called Grace?"

"Grace?" repeated Monica. "Grace, yes, she's my friend. In fact, I saw her yesterday in the café in town. I went in hoping some tea and a bun would cheer me up, but it didn't. Grace called in."

Gardener was pleased that Monica was far more forthcoming than Grace was when Gates and Longstaff questioned her on the same subject.

"How long have you known her?" asked Gardener.

Monica appeared to think again. "Let me see. Not all that long, she's a relatively new friend, maybe three or four months. You can't tell me *she's* been robbing the post offices."

That thought brought another smile to Gardener's face as he tried to picture the scene.

"How did you two meet?" asked Reilly.

"That's a day I remember all too well," said Monica. "I was having a real off day, with the Addison's, you know. God, I was dead on my feet. I shouldn't even have been driving." She stopped and put her hands to her mouth. "Should I have said that? It probably was an offence."

"Don't worry, love," said Reilly. "We're nothing to do with traffic."

Monica smiled, appeared relieved, and continued.

"Trouble is, I'd been working ridiculous shifts and I had nothing in the house. I desperately needed to do a food shop. I remember being on the point of collapse. Bloody stupid really, I shouldn't have done it."

"Needs must, Monica, love," said Reilly. "You have to live, and you don't strike me as the type to give in."

"I'm not. You can't, can you? Otherwise, what's the point? Anyway, I was actually on the verge of collapse when Grace appeared and asked if I was okay, and could she help me? She could see I wasn't well. I still didn't want to accept help, but I honestly couldn't see another way round it. She was a bloody angel, I'll give her that. She actually drove me home in my car, helped me into the house, put all my shopping away, made some tea, sat with me, made sure I'd settled down, and taken my medication. I did actually start to feel better."

Gardener wondered what in God's name was going on with Grace. How much did she actually know about everything? And how much was she telling them?

"How did she get back home?"

"Caught a taxi back to the supermarket, and then drove to her own place in her own car, I assume."

"Very spirited of her," said Reilly.

"And I'll tell you something else, she would not take any money for helping. I even offered to pay for the taxi back, but she wouldn't take that. She was an angel that day."

"So it's fair to say you've become good friends?" asked Gardener.

"How could we not, after that?" said Monica. "What surprised me was that she called me the next day to see how I was, and we arranged to meet for coffee when I was feeling better."

"Why did it surprise you?" asked Reilly.

"Because I can't remember giving her my number," said Monica. "I suppose she could have asked the taxi firm for it because it was me who suggested calling them."

"But would they give her your number?" asked Reilly. "Data protection, and all that?"

"I never thought of that," said Monica.

"How well would you say you know her?" Gardener asked.

Monica thought again. "Now that you ask, probably not all that well. I know she lives in Bursley Bridge, but I've never been there."

"Does she come here often?" asked Reilly.

"I think she's been about three or four times. Last week was the last time."

"What day?" Gardener asked.

"I'm not sure if it was Thursday or Friday." Monica suddenly stood up and checked a slim wall calendar. "It was Friday," she said, before taking a seat again. "It's pretty easy for her to arrange things, what with her being single."

"Single?" repeated Gardener.

"Yes, single," replied Monica. "Sounds like she has the life of Riley." Glancing at the sergeant, she said, "No pun intended."

He laughed.

"Anyway, what is all this about? Why are you questioning me about Grace? She surely hasn't done anything wrong."

"Depends how you define wrong," said Reilly.

"Has she?" asked Monica, her expression shocked.

"Would it surprise you to know that her surname is Challenger?"

"Challenger?" said Monica. "As in, Davey?"

Gardener nodded.

"Is she his sister? He never mentioned having one."

"No," said Reilly.

"Well who is she, then? She certainly can't be his mother."

"His wife," said Reilly.

Monica's expression wavered, and her mouth fell open. "Wife?"

"I'm afraid so," said Gardener.

"Wait a minute," said Monica. "She's his wife? But Davey wasn't married."

"I'm afraid he was," said Reilly.

She stood up and then sat down equally as quickly, tears flowing freely.

"What the hell is going on here? Why would she try and make friends with me, knowing full well I was having an affair with her husband?"

"That's what we'd like to know," said Gardener.

Monica's mood changed. "I just don't believe this. I didn't think things could get any worse, and now this. At least I know who will be organising his funeral. I've worried about that since I heard. And why the hell did he leave me everything in his will?" Monica went off at a tangent. She was obviously seething. "You just bloody well wait till I see her again. I've a good mind to bloody well drive over there now."

"Where?" asked Gardener.

"To her house."

"Which is where?"

Monica stopped, admitting she didn't actually know. "Oh my God, what a cruel bloody game."

"We'd prefer you not to have any further contact with her, Miss Rushby, until we can piece everything together. If she does contact you, please don't respond. Speak to us first."

"I somehow doubt she will, after all this," said Monica.

"When you say he left you everything in his will, what exactly is everything?" asked Gardener.

"Not a lot, really," replied Monica. "Some small personal items of jewellery. He also left me money."

"How much?" asked Reilly.

"Fifteen thousand."

Gardener wondered how Challenger had come by that much, if, as Grace claimed, she was the one holding all the financial cards. It would have to be the proceeds of the last robbery. When he suddenly showed up and shot his gun, leaving the other two empty-handed.

"If you don't mind me asking," said Gardener, "how was the money left to you?"

"I'm not really sure, but I haven't got it yet, so it certainly isn't in cash."

"May we have the details of the solicitor, please?" Gardener asked.

Monica Rushby found a pad and pen and wrote the details down, and then went on the attack again.

"Has she known all along? Just what kind of a game is she playing?"

Gardener never answered, he didn't have time to.

"Has she set me up?" asked Monica. "Is she claiming that I poisoned her husband, because I work in a hospital and have access to drugs?"

Gardener still chose not to answer.

"She has, hasn't she? She's been no friend of mine. She's wanted to set me up. But why? Okay, I know I was having an affair with her husband, and trust me, if I'd have known, I wouldn't have touched him with a bargepole."

She stopped but then started again.

"What does she gain from this?" Her eyes widened. "Oh my God! Is it the will, does it give me a motive? And the results of the autopsy report have played right into her hands. What a conniving cow! And to think, I thought she was my friend."

Monica checked her cup, found it empty. She stood and moved to the sink and then broke down in floods of tears.

"Mr Gardener," she said, between sobs. "I don't know what's been implied, or what's been said, but I want you to know that I did not kill Davey, nor did I have anything to do with the robberies."

Gardener felt for her. But he wasn't stupid. Even though Monica had a motive, he and his sergeant were still struggling to put her directly in place, for two reasons: her strong alibis and the fact that before coming to see Monica, the pair of them spent an hour at the hospital pharmacy checking all the stock; everything was in order.

But in order to dot all the i's and cross all the t's, Gardener still had to ask Monica for a list of all the medication she was taking in order to rule out whether anything she had at home could have been converted into aconitine.

Chapter Thirty-one

It was almost nine in the evening when Gates and Longstaff pulled up outside Dominic Appleby's house on Haygate Lane. The sun had gone down on another warm day, offering a clear but chilly night. As they left the car, Gates glanced upwards.

"Might have a ground frost in the morning," she said to Longstaff.

"Promising another nice day, though." Longstaff stopped, and then said, "Isn't this what you talk about when you get old?"

"Or married," said Gates.

"God forbid either," said Longstaff.

Gates glanced at the detached house in front of them; it had a standard brick exterior and PVC double-glazed windows. She could see lights on in a couple of the rooms. In front of a double garage, she saw what she thought was a Ford Mustang with the registration D1 ABY. Stocks and shares must pay quite well, she thought.

As they approached the porch, a carriage lamp lit up, and before she could ring the doorbell, Appleby answered. He was dressed in a sweatshirt, jeans and slippers, and his hair appeared damp, as if he had recently stepped out of the shower, but despite that he still had a five o'clock shadow.

"Thank you for coming over," he said.

"Sorry we couldn't make it any earlier," said Gates.

"Oh, don't worry."

Appleby ushered them inside, through a warmly decorated hallway with regency striped wallpaper and thick carpeting underfoot. He then led them into a living room that was minimal and perhaps not to everyone's taste. The furniture was a very modern mixture of leather and chrome, which appeared as uncomfortable as hell to Gates, with wall units that bent in all directions, and because of the combination of those two, nothing in the room appeared to be straight. Gates was pleased she wasn't drunk. She could, however, hear a surround sound system to die for.

"I've switched off for the night," said Appleby. "Hence the drink." He pointed to a tumbler on the coffee table. "Brandy and lemonade. Can I fix a drink for either of you two?"

"Love one," said Longstaff. "But we're on duty, I'm afraid."

"Bit of a pain, wouldn't you say?"

"Can be," said Gates.

"Okay. You can still have a drink. Would you prefer warm or cold?"

Both girls said a coffee would be nice. He told them to take a seat and returned a minute later with two cups from a percolator that he said had been freshly brewed about fifteen minutes before they arrived. "You said you thought you had something important to tell us regarding the case," Longstaff said.

"I'm not sure if it is, really, but then don't they say any information could prove valuable?"

"You've no idea," said Gates.

"It's just that I keep thinking back to the morning I found the van on fire," said Appleby. "I always jog the same route and it came to me that twice in the last couple of weeks I've seen the same car."

"Where?" Gates asked.

"On Haygate Lane."

"Going which way?" asked Longstaff.

"Back toward the town."

"You've never seen it on East Ings Lane?"

"No," he replied.

"Did you recognise the car?"

"No, I've only seen it here, and very early in the morning," said Appleby. "I mean it could be anything. Might be a social worker visiting an elderly patient."

"Can't remember the registration, can you?" asked Gates.

"No," said Appleby. "It's not something you look at when you're running. Unless it's hit you, in which case that would be the last thing you see."

Both ladies found the funny side of that one.

"The only thing I noticed was the female driver."

"Female?" said Gates. "Did you recognise her?"

"No. Again, not easy at that time of the morning because you often have to contend with a glare on the windscreen, so you can't really see anything."

"What colour was the car?" asked Longstaff.

"Purple."

Gates nodded. "That could narrow things down. There will certainly be a number of manufacturers that *don't* produce a purple car."

"Could be a Fiat," offered Longstaff. "They're popular in purple."

"Anything outstanding about the car?" asked Gates. "Did it have stripes, or maybe even a dented panel?"

"Not that I can remember," said Appleby, taking a sip of his drink.

"Have you ever seen it anywhere else around the town?"

He thought about the question. "No, can't say I have, but to be honest I work from home, and there are weeks on end that I don't even go out. I shop online and most of that gets delivered."

Gates was beginning to think it was a wasted journey. Admittedly he'd told them something they didn't know but it would be of little help to them.

As she was about to finish her coffee and wrap things up, Appleby said, "But, I can do a bit better than that."

"How do you mean?" Longstaff asked.

His phone pinged, which distracted everyone's attention. He surprised Gates when he simply ignored it.

"Well, I don't know if you noticed but I have CCTV cameras perched on the side of the house. It usually records for a week and then everything is erased but before that happens I save it to my hard drive and date it." He chuckled. "I bet you think I'm a right plank, don't you? Locked up here in this place day after day with only my computers to keep me happy, recording and dating my CCTV."

"You'd be surprised what we come across," said Longstaff. "You're okay, at least you can hold a conversation. Most people in IT, or those who spend a lot of time on their phones, have no social skills whatsoever."

"You're telling me," said Gates. "You know, we sent out for pizza last night. I was rushing around as usual so I ordered for me and Graham and then I passed the phone to Sophie to order one for her and one for her brother. She wouldn't talk to him. Completely blanked me and almost ran out of the room, all because she didn't want to talk to someone. What's that all about?"

Appleby and Longstaff laughed.

"Did she get a pizza, then?" asked Appleby.

"Oh yeah," said Gates, laughing. "But she had to bloody well eat what I ordered for her. That'll teach her."

After they all found it amusing, Gates returned Appleby to the CCTV.

"Yes." He jumped up and strolled over to the hi-fi unit, slid open a drawer in a cabinet underneath and brought a USB stick back to a laptop at the side of the TV. "It's all on here. You can take it with you, but I thought you might want to see it before you go. See whether or not you think it's important."

He inserted the stick. Gates noticed he had segregated the files and dated them, as he'd said. As they watched, two of the files simply showed the small purple car in question. They had to take his word for it that it was purple because the CCTV was black and white. Gates noted that one of the times was around eight in the evening, and another was around lunchtime, three days apart.

More importantly however was the file dated March 26th, in the early hours of the morning; that was the one that made the hairs of the nape of Gates' neck bristle.

The footage actually showed a van – which had to be the one they were investigating – being driven past his house at three-thirty. Two minutes later, the same small purple car followed the van. Because it was a side view, you could not see the registration plate. But Gates wasn't so worried because she had what she thought was solid gold on file. The techs would almost certainly be able to do something with it.

The footage then showed the little purple car return down Haygate Lane an hour later – on its own – passing Appleby's house, going in the opposite direction, heading toward the town.

"Interesting," said Longstaff. "And that *is* the same purple car you've seen while you were jogging?"

"Yes."

Gates asked him to run it back three or four times to see if she could spot anything out of the ordinary. She couldn't, but she felt confident the techs could enhance the footage and if there was something specific, there was a very good chance they might have their man, so to speak.

"Excellent," said Gates, taking the USB that was on offer.

"Do you think it might all be relevant?" asked Appleby.

"It certainly looks promising," said Gates.

"You will let me know if anything comes of it, won't you?"

"Definitely," said Gates. "Good work, Mr Appleby."

"See," said Longstaff, smiling, "staying at home does have its advantages."

Chapter Thirty-two

Thursday morning in the incident room, Gardener was very keen to talk about what Gates and Longstaff had found following their visit to Dominic Appleby, amongst other things.

His first subject was the Shell station in Birmingham, which had yet to deliver any results on the CCTV. Gardener asked for the number and said that he personally would put a rocket up them.

Which brought him around to two subjects that definitely needed further discussion and input from the team.

"Grace Challenger," said Gardener, standing to the left of the whiteboard. "The girls visited her yesterday because she had called in saying she had found something important – her husband's mobile phone."

"Where the hell was that?" asked Anderson.

"In the garage, apparently," said Longstaff.

"Haven't we searched that place?" asked Thornton.

"Where in the garage?" asked Gardener.

"The word she used first, was hidden," said Longstaff. "But then she said that it wasn't really hidden, she happened to come across it on a shelf."

"Any idea why she was in the garage?" asked Reilly. "What was she looking for?"

"We never actually asked," said Gates. "But we placed a call to the SOCOs and asked if they could seal the place off and do a deep search."

"Something about this isn't running to form," said Gardener. "Steve Fenton's guys have searched that place already. I don't believe they would make such a schoolboy error. Furthermore, they handed the scene over to us when they'd finished, which suggests they *had* made a thorough check. I'll call Steve Fenton after we've finished here."

"I get the feeling this Grace one knows more than she's letting on," said Reilly.

"I know what you mean, Sean," said Gardener. "I don't particularly think she was involved in either the robbery, the murder, or setting fire to the van but…"

"You think she knows something?" asked Sharp.

"Definitely," said Gardener. "Take Monica Rushby for example. Grace claims she was a friend of the woman her husband was having an affair with. I don't buy that."

"No," said Anderson. "That sounds to me like she found out about the affair and decided to befriend the Rushby woman so she could carry out some kind of warped revenge."

"I'm inclined to agree," said Gardener. "As for everything we're looking into, I certainly don't have her down for a post office robbery, but *is* she capable of murder?"

"Or framing someone else for it?" asked Reilly.

"Can we verify her alibis?" asked Rawson.

"Not really," said Gardener. "To me, the most important would be the night of her husband's murder. She says she was home alone. She may have been, but we have no way of proving it."

"I also get the impression," said Longstaff, "that she's putting on her emotions. We saw her yesterday and she reached for the tissues a bit too often."

"She has just lost her husband," said Benson.

"Granted," said Gates. "But her body language and her mannerisms don't portray that. Every time anyone sees her, and we've all interviewed her, she looks ten million dollars."

"Unlike Monica Rushby," said Gardener. "No disrespect to the woman but she looked terrible yesterday. I really don't believe she is in on anything, either; her alibis hold up, and her emotions *are* all over the place."

"She was spitting barbed wire yesterday," said Reilly. "When we told her exactly who Grace Challenger was."

"I think we need to take a closer look at Grace Challenger," said Gardener. "Check her bank movements. I know we've been through her husband's and everything appears normal there, but I want hers checking, see if there is any abnormal behaviour, large transfers in or out."

"You're not thinking the post office money, are you, sir?" asked Patrick Edwards.

"It has to have gone somewhere, Patrick," said Gardener. "Although to be honest, I don't think Grace Challenger is stupid enough to start moving large sums of money through her bank account. I think Sean and I are going to pay another visit to Grace, see if we can shake her enough to let something slip out."

Gardener made a note and then turned his attention to Appleby's information.

"This is really good news."

The SIO had everything set up and he played the footage that Gates and Longstaff had collected. The team watched at least three times, all agreeing it was helpful, but it didn't have any money shots – as in a registration.

"No," said Gardener, "but at least we have something. I'm pretty certain that was our van. Let's run it through again and double check the times."

They documented the van and the small car going past Appleby's house at three-thirty in the morning. The little car then returned alone one hour later at four-thirty.

Gardener added notes to the whiteboard and then said, "Let's have the tech team on it, see if they can come up with something more definitive on that car."

"I can tell you what that is," said Sharp. "It's a Suzuki, and if I'm not mistaken, it's a Swift."

"Well done, Colin," said Gardener. "How do you know that?"

"My wife used to have one. Sod all swift about them, that's all I can say."

Following more laughter, and banter about second-rate cars, Gardener continued.

"Okay, we have something to go on here. I realize these views are sideways on and at some distance, but we might be able to enhance the footage enough to see who is driving the vehicles, particularly the Swift."

"Dominic Appleby claims he's seen it two of three times," said Gates, "mostly in the same area. He also claims that a woman was driving. I think this is going to be an important bit of information."

"I agree," said Gardener. "If it does turn out to be a Swift then we should get on to Suzuki, see if they can help – tell us how many were sold in this area and to whom. Colour will be the all-important factor. That should narrow it down a little more."

Gardener turned his attention to the van.

"Now that we have our first real view of this thing before it was set on fire, we may have a little more luck with the CCTV around the town. Anything come up yet?"

"Nothing so far," said Gates. "But to be honest, we turned our attention to Challenger's phone once we had it, and we do have something interesting."

"Do tell," said Gardener.

"We've discovered that a text was placed to a number that was coded on his phone," said Gates.

"Coded?" asked Gardener.

"There were two," said Longstaff. "You know the kind of thing. If someone's up to no good, in order to avoid detection they will put different names into their phones, their pet's name, or a character from a film."

"Anyway," continued Gates, "we know that one of them is Monica's number. The second however is something totally different. We've done some digging with the phone companies. Turns out that one was placed to none other than our crazy little horse specialist, Frankie."

"What did the text actually say?" asked Gardener.

"Just two words: *all yours*."

There was a short silence as the information sunk in.

Longstaff took over. "That text was placed on the morning Challenger died" – she checked her notes – "at 4.15 am."

"4.15," repeated Gardener. "Who the hell sent that, then?"

"Maybe Challenger himself," offered Reilly. "It's possible that he was still alive at that point. Maybe that was the plan: do the robbery, let the heat die down, and then torch the van somewhere remote."

"But somebody else thought different," said Sharp. "Sounds like the third person involved in the robberies might have known all along that Frankie and Challenger were shafting him."

"But why get rid of Challenger and not Frankie?" asked Gardener.

"Maybe Frankie *is* responsible for killing Challenger," said Rawson. "Perhaps the two of them had a plan but Frankie double-crossed Challenger. The plan was for Challenger to offload the van, and for Frankie to come and torch it. After all, he doesn't live that far away."

"Too many people to do one simple job," said Gardener. "If that had been the case it would have been easier for Challenger to do it all. Reclaim the van from where he'd hidden it, drive it to the field and torch it."

"Does make more sense," said Reilly.

"Interesting, but what does it mean?" asked Benson.

"That whoever killed Challenger was working *with* Frankie," said Gardener. "I think that message was meant to relay that Challenger was dead, and the van was in place."

"For Frankie to torch?" asked Rawson.

"That's how it appears to me," said Gardener.

"We have something else," said Gates.

She worked her way through the phone and finally allowed them to listen to a couple of conversations, that also appeared coded, but they definitely put Davey Challenger in the picture for the last post office robbery, where someone ended up badly injured when he pulled the trigger.

The person talking to Challenger sounded like Frankie. No other names were mentioned, and the conversation was mostly about how the fourth robbery would pan out.

"Challenger sounds very unsettled," said Gardener, "as if he was well out of his league."

"Either that, or the fact that he was having to work with that idiot, Frankie," said Reilly.

"Would have been nice if one of them had mentioned the third elusive person in all of this," said Anderson.

"Well, I'm pretty sure we'll soon find that out," said Gardener. "Pull that little scrote Frankie in. *We* can push him to reveal the identity of the third person."

"I think you can do that one on your own, boss," said Reilly. "His breath nearly killed us the other day and we were outside."

Gardener smiled. "Maybe it's time Patrick learned about interviewing techniques."

"Oh, thanks, boss."

"Don't worry, Patrick," said Gardener. "Thanks to Covid we all have to wear masks in the interview suites now."

"Could the third person be Mitchell?" asked Reilly.

"Anything's possible," said Rawson. "He's down there out of the way, miles from anywhere. It's a great cover for sorting out all sorts of dodgy business."

"It's not the impression *we* got of Mitchell," said Benson, relaying all the good words his neighbours had for him.

"If it isn't," said Gardener, "maybe that's because Mitchell's business is legit, and Frankie is riding around on the back of it. He's the one doing all the dodgy deals behind Mitchell's back, using Mitchell's reputation as a guarantee."

"I'm not sure Mitchell is that stupid," said Reilly.

"Either way," said Gardener, "we *will* have to talk to him. If he is completely legit, and he is the saint his neighbours claim him to be, he won't be too happy to hear about this."

"Which also leads us back to another unanswered question," said Reilly. "Who has the money from the post office jobs?"

"Frankie is a possibility," said Gardener. "Do you remember us talking to Mitchell at the start of this investigation? He told us that Frankie had money dotted all over the yard. We have to look much closer into that because I can't see Mitchell paying him a fortune."

"Don't forget the horses," said Reilly.

"Surely he can't win that much," said Longstaff.

"According to Mitchell he does," said Gardener. "He's been banned from all the local bookies for fleecing them." Gardener turned to Benson, knowing he was into horses. "What do you think, Paul?"

"It has been known, sir, but if he's that good, the chances are he's getting inside information from someone."

"Either way," said Gardener, "we need the man in here. Colin, Dave, can you two pop down to the scrapyard and bring this little toerag in? Also, have a word with Mitchell, and see what you can pick up from him, particularly about the money."

Gardener turned to Maurice Cragg and asked him what he knew of the people mentioned.

"I know 'em all," said Cragg. "None of them have any previous to my knowledge. I'm really surprised that

Challenger has turned out criminal. Like I said previously, local lad, never in any trouble as a youngster, or an adult. Married a bit out of his class, which might be one reason for it all. He was trying to keep Grace to the life to which she was accustomed.

"Mitchell is also a local lad, and I get what you're saying about him being out of the way, but nothing has ever come to light about him. He always appears to have kept his nose clean, so he might surprise me as well.

"As for the other shape, Frankie. The only reason I can't see him being involved is because if brains were dynamite, he wouldn't have enough to blow his nose. I think the only reason Mitchell employs him is because no one else will. Mitchell feels sorry for him."

"Okay," said Gardener. "Some really good work from all of you. I think we're moving ever closer to finding out what really happened here, but we can't relax. Keep at it, tying up the loose ends will prove important."

Gardener turned to Cragg. "Any news on the postmaster, George Spencer?"

"Still the same, sir," replied Cragg.

Chapter Thirty-three

Sharp brought the car to a halt at the end of East Ings Lane and both he and Rawson jumped out. It was another cracking day, Sharp observed, barely a cloud to spoil the sun. Closing the doors, the pair of them entered the yard to find it deserted.

"Christ," said Rawson. "It's a few years since I've seen a place like this."

"Know what you mean," said Sharp, glancing at the hundreds of cars strewn everywhere, some of them three high. "It's a health and safety nightmare. Do you think he really knows what he has in here?"

"Down to the last car," replied Rawson, laughing, peering left and right.

"Do you know," said Sharp, "when I was younger these were the places to be. There were quite a few in Leeds, and when me and me mates all started driving, we used to pop in every week. You'd come for a suspension arm, or another big item, but you never left with empty pockets. I had all sorts stashed away: ignition parts, wiper blades. I once had an air filter stuffed up my jumper. Do you reckon they knew… what was going on?"

Rawson laughed out loud. "Of course they did, they're not daft. Mind you, saying that, I caught one of them out big style a few years back."

"What happened?"

"I remember going to a yard where they were welding the front of one car to the back of another – a cut and shut job, to try to make one good car," said Rawson. "It was sitting in a back shed and I asked the owner – who had much bigger problems to worry about – why it wasn't finished." Rawson started laughing out loud. "He said, the daft beggars had welded the back end of a sporty model with flared arches to the front end of a base model, which didn't have them. It looked like a hot wheels car – totally out of proportion.

"But I'll tell you what we did find; a load of scrap metal copper pipes in there, filled with sand, and some paper stuffed in either end to stop the sand dropping out. I asked him why, and he said they weigh it in at their rival's yard and get a lot more for it because the sand makes it heavier."

As the pair of them laughed, a voice behind said, "Oldest trick in the book."

"Oh, sorry, mate," said Sharp, flashing his warrant card. "We're looking for Frankie."

"You just missed him, but maybe I can help you with something. I'm Derrick Mitchell."

"If you don't mind answering a few questions," said Rawson.

"No," said Mitchell. "Come on through."

He led them into the portacabin and showed them both a seat. Standing near a percolator he asked if they wanted coffee. Both said they would.

When they were all seated, Rawson asked where Frankie was and what time he was due back.

"He'll not be back when he should be. It *was* quiet this morning, but then we had a call came in about a couple of scrappers from a bloke across Morecambe way, so I sent him off."

"Fair distance," said Sharp. "Does it pay, going all that way?"

"Ordinarily, no," said Mitchell. "But I had some stuff needed delivering that way so I thought I might as well kill two birds with one stone."

"You are expecting him back today?" asked Rawson.

"Any normal person, yes, I would," said Mitchell, taking a sip of coffee. "But this is Frankie we're talking about. He'll make a day of it, find a few bookies, make himself a packet."

"Yes," said Rawson. "We heard about that. I must have a word with him sometime."

"You should. He gave one of your bosses a tip the other day and it romped home; should have earned him a packet. Anyway, what do you want him for?"

"We really need to ask him a few more questions in connection with the van fire," said Sharp. "What do you know about him?"

Mitchell rolled his eyes. "Jesus, if I'm being truthful, very little."

"How long has he worked for you?"

"Now you're asking," replied Mitchell, who scratched his head, as if it might help. "About five years, I reckon."

"Where was he from originally?" asked Rawson.

"That's a really good question, and I'm gonna sound stupid, but I have no idea."

Sharp glanced at Rawson, wondering what the set-up was. "You don't keep records, then?" he asked Mitchell.

"Usually, yes, but not with him; you can't get a straight answer out of him."

"So how did you actually meet?"

"That's another strange one," said Mitchell. "I remember having to pop out one day. I forget what I was doing but whatever it was, it took far longer than expected. When I got back, there were a few punters in the yard, all studying vehicles. Anyway, I left 'em to it, made myself a cuppa and came back out. I remember seeing Frankie, head inside an engine bay, as if it was eating him.

"When he straightened up he gave some part to this bloke and pointed in my direction. Bloke came over, said my mechanic had taken it off for him and asked how much I wanted. I said, my mechanic? He said, yes, that little fella over there. By this time, he was helping someone else out.

"Anyway, once I'd taken this bloke's money, I decided to leave the little fella to it – see how long it lasted. He was still here at seven, happily stripping bits off cars. Eventually I went to talk to him, and he said he liked messing with cars and wondered if I needed any help. I didn't, but he looked like he was on his uppers so I said, yes, I'll give you a trial. He's been here ever since."

"And is that what he does, strip cars?" asked Sharp.

"Sometimes. I'll give him one thing, he definitely knows his way around them. But mostly nowadays, he goes driving for me. He's pretty good at it. Never hit anything. He usually gets back late, but to be honest it's *his* time – no one's chasing him."

"Ever seen his licence?" asked Rawson.

Mitchell held his hands up. "It's a scrapyard. I never really intended him to drive for me, and when he got round to it, I didn't think to ask. Guilty, officer."

"And you've never asked him where he came from?" asked Rawson. "Or anything else about him?"

"No," said Mitchell. "Never came up. All I know is, he's reliable and pretty loyal, and I don't have to pay him much, and what I do pay him, is cash."

"Does he have any family?" asked Sharp.

Mitchell spread his arms. "Like I said, gentlemen, I have no idea."

"Is it true he lives here?" asked Rawson.

Mitchell laughed. "Yes, in a bloody monstrosity of a caravan. He was in a makeshift shelter before that. I came across it one day, wondered what the hell it was. As I was staring at it, trying to work it out, he stepped through the flap. Apparently he'd been living there since that first day. It was a month before I noticed."

"Do you send him all over, collecting cars?" asked Sharp.

"That's right," said Mitchell. "It's easier now, with satnavs. Poor old Frankie is dyslexic. Before them things he might be missing for a week."

They all laughed.

"Is it possible that you recently sent him to Birmingham?"

"I could have done," said Mitchell. "Do you have a particular date?"

Sharp supplied it. Mitchell checked, and then confirmed he did, which very possibly cleared up another little mystery.

"Does he ever buy things and return the receipts?" asked Rawson.

"Not always," said Mitchell, but seeing as they'd asked, he checked the receipts for that day. There wasn't anything for petrol from a fuel station on New Street, though that didn't mean anything.

Mitchell sat back down.

"These questions are little bit pointed. If you don't mind me asking, what's going on?"

Sharp ignored the question for the time being and asked one of his own.

"When our boss came around the other day, you mentioned the piles of money that Frankie has stashed away."

Mitchell laughed. "His winnings?"

"Is that what it is?" asked Rawson. "Does he really win all that on the horses?"

"A lot of it comes from the horses."

"Any idea what else he's wrapped up in that could earn him that kind of money?"

"Nothing that *I* really know of. I know he does odd jobs for people around the town but that wouldn't earn him the kind of money he has stashed away. We have to remember, he's been backing horses most of his life, and if he was winning then like he is now, then maybe that's why he has a lot."

"And he keeps it hidden around the yard?"

"Most of it," said Mitchell. "Well, probably all of it. He might even have a lot I *don't* know about."

"He might even be *into* a lot that you don't know about," suggested Rawson.

"I wouldn't have thought so, officer," said Mitchell. "It's a small town, there's always someone who knows your business, and who would be only too happy to split on you."

Sharp brought the subject of the robberies up. He supplied Mitchell with the dates and asked where Frankie was on those days. For purposes of elimination, they also asked where he was.

Mitchell checked and said as far as he could tell they were in the yard on each of those dates – himself and Frankie.

"I realize it's not much of an alibi but it's the best I can offer," said Mitchell. "However, on each of those dates I did spend a bit of time away from the yard, so I'll write down where I was, and you can check it out."

"So if you had business away from the yard," said Rawson, "is it possible Frankie may have slipped out in your absence?"

"You're right, he could have, and I wouldn't be able to prove it one way or another."

"What about your CCTV?" asked Sharp.

Mitchell snorted and laughed. "That pile of crap. It works when it wants and mostly it doesn't."

"How often do you check it?" asked Sharp.

"Never, if I'm honest."

"How often does it get wiped?"

"If we remember to use it, every couple of days." Mitchell stood up and checked his computer. "Look at that, according to this, the last time it was set was the beginning of March."

"All the same," said Sharp. "Can we have the back-up copies to check through?"

"Of course. How far back do you want to go?"

"Six months max," said Sharp.

"Okay, let me sort through it today and I'll get copies to you tonight."

As he sat back down, Mitchell's expression suddenly changed – his features pinched, and his eyes narrowed.

"I've just thought of something, you're not asking about all this, his money and such, because you think he's the one who's turned over those post offices, are you?"

"Would it surprise you if he had?" asked Rawson.

Mitchell appeared stunned. "It'd fucking paralyze me. Frankie is far too stupid to get in on anything like that. No one would employ him. He's too much of a liability, especially when he's had a drink."

"Why do *you* employ him?" asked Sharp.

"Probably because I like to give people a chance. And as I said, he's handy, and pretty loyal."

"Okay," said Sharp, "I think I'll leave it at that, but if you could have him contact us when he gets back, we'd like a word with him."

"I will," said Mitchell.

As Sharp stood, he turned to Mitchell. "Before we go, do you mind if we have a look around the yard? As I said to my colleague earlier, I spent my Saturday afternoons in places like this. It would bring back some good memories."

"Be my guest."

As they left, Mitchell sat back down, thinking. What in God's name was going on with Frankie?

Whatever it was, he needed to find out, for Terry's sake.

Chapter Thirty-four

Frankie was propping up the bar of The Royal Inn, Bramfield. He'd had one hell of a day and was currently in one of the best moods he'd been in for some time.

He'd finished the Morecambe gig in record time, having arrived back in town by mid-afternoon. He'd seen no reason to go back to the yard. Mitchell would have found him something else to do. Frankie had been far too loaded to think about work.

Whilst in Morecambe he had checked out all the bookies. He'd found four of them reasonably close together, approximately within six streets of each other. In the space of a couple of hours he had turned two hundred pounds into three thousand. Once he'd collected his winnings, he shot out of Dodge rather quickly.

Back in Bramfield he had parked the low-loader in a side street and sought out The Royal Inn – a traditional establishment with wooden tables and chairs, a jukebox, a dartboard, and a pool table; only slightly higher up the ladder from a spit and sawdust saloon, which suited Frankie.

Sitting at the table, his mouth had been watering. The waitress gave him a menu, which was a complete waste of time. Frankie preferred menus with pictures, so he could point to the meal. Not that it always helped, he'd been surprised on more than one occasion, particularly when he once sat waiting for a massive bowl of spaghetti bolognaise, only to be served beans on toast. Hadn't been a problem, he'd used them as a starter.

To supplement his lack of reading knowledge he often asked the waitress what she recommended. Today, she said soap and water would be a good choice. Frankie didn't know what the hell she was on about. He'd eaten most shit but he'd never tried that. He said he'd pass and start with soup of the day – two bowls. Normal or washing-up bowls, she'd asked. He'd laughed but didn't know what at.

He'd followed that with the biggest steak they had, and all the trimmings: chips, mushrooms, onion rings, to which he'd also added sausages and an egg, for the top of the steak. The waitress had thought he was joking – her expression had said as much. After that it was trifle. He'd then asked for a cheeseboard. He didn't think the waitress had taken him seriously because she'd asked him more than once if he was sure he wanted that much, probably wondering whether or not he had the means to pay. All of that had been washed down with six pints of best bitter.

After the meal, and the paying of the bill, he waddled to the bar in the back room where it was a little quieter. This meant he could burp and fart till his heart was content.

Someone had eventually asked Frankie if he'd wanted to make up the darts team. It wouldn't have been a good idea even had Frankie been sober. He remembered the last time he had made the numbers up. On the point of taking his first shot, some bastard shouted at him. Startled, Frankie turned to see whom. At that point the dart actually left his hand. Most people found it funny, but not so amusing for the bloke whose eye he had nearly removed.

Whilst he was reminiscing, a punter entered the small room, strolled up to the bar and fished around for his money. The barman took his order, and Frankie overheard the man say that he'd had a cracking day on the horses, and thought it was worth celebrating.

"Oh, hey," said Frankie, putting his thumb in the air.

At the mention of horses, he became all ears. That and the fact that he was now seven or eight pints in – he was fucked if he could remember how many, or who was counting – meant he was anybody's anyway. Horses were the bonus.

"Sorry," said the man.

He was around six feet tall, dressed in jeans and Barbour jacket and good quality leather boots. His face was tanned and wrinkled, and he sported a trimmed moustache and beard, which matched his grey hair.

"Good day," slurred Frankie, "on the nags."

"Oh, yes." The man smiled. "Had a couple of good winners, made a few quid."

"Same here," said Frankie.

"You as well? How many?"

"Four."

"Pardon?" said the man.

"Four," repeated Frankie, "all winners. Made a packet."

"Oh." The man nodded. "Better than me."

As the landlord returned, Frankie held out a crisp twenty-pound note. "On me. And one for yourself, sir."

The man picked up his pint and nodded to Frankie. "That's very good of you, thank you."

With both drinks served and change left on the bar, Frankie bid him good health and asked what he did. The man introduced himself as Norman Darkman, and said he was a simple farmer.

Norman then asked what Frankie was into.

Frankie laughed and wobbled and said something that even he hadn't understood, never mind the farmer. The stool rocked and Frankie grabbed the bar to steady himself and farted at the same time, then he pulled himself back to the bar and laughed again in Norman's direction. The farmer tipped backwards, and blinked aggressively, as if he'd been hit by a missile, before turning slightly.

"Close one," said Frankie.

"On more than one account," said Norman.

A little time passed and the farmer asked, "Good with the horses, are you, my friend?"

Frankie rolled his head and his eyes a few times, moved his hands in all directions and then actually said, "Not bad."

"I've heard that said before by people like you and next thing you know they're millionaires."

"Aye," said Frankie, laughing, ordering more drinks.

Norman pulled out a *Racing Post* from the inside of his jacket and waved it in front of Frankie's face.

"How do you fancy picking tomorrow's winners?"

Frankie moved backwards and forwards in an effort to bring the *paper* into focus, never mind the print. There was no chance with that. He couldn't read it for all the tea in China.

He made a real show of trying to find his non-existent glasses, and then dropped in a bit of a weak excuse that he was going to siphon the python, and if farmer Giles wanted to lay the paper out they would have a browse when Frankie returned.

Which, to everyone's surprise, after five minutes he actually managed to find his way back into the room without the use of the satnav.

Back on the stool, Frankie squinted at the paper, which was swimming in and out of focus. Farmer Giles would have been better asking the horse to read it.

"Okay," said Frankie.

"Okay, what?" asked Norman.

"Read out the race meetings and give me the form."

"You don't want much, do you?" said Norman.

"No, but you do."

Norman seemed to find that funny and read out the first race. When he'd finished he said, "Mighty Atom, seven to one."

"No," said Frankie.

"Go on then, brain of Britain, tell me what you think."

Frankie laughed, and nearly fell off his stool, causing an Earth tremor. Once he'd regained his balance, he quickly said, "The Bruiser."

Norman studied it. "Are you serious? It's fifty to one."

Frankie simply nodded and repeated, "The Bruiser."

Norman reluctantly made a note, and after that they spent another hour drinking and talking and Frankie couldn't remember any of the conversation. Eventually, the farmer dragged another newspaper from the inside of his coat and studied the lead story.

"Bad business, this," said Norman, eventually.

"Things will pick up," replied Frankie, glancing around the bar.

"I didn't mean that."

Frankie turned back. "What did you mean?"

"This," said Norman.

Frankie squinted at the paper again, as if he was studying it through the long end of a telescope, which might have been better for him.

"Sorry, haven't brought me glasses."

"Oh, sorry," said Norman. "So you said earlier. This business with the post office robberies, it's bloody terrible. You're not safe nowadays."

Frankie started wobbling and chuckling. The stool started rocking and bouncing.

"I could tell you some stories about them."

"What?" Norman asked. "The robberies?"

Frankie grabbed his left ear. "Keep this to the ground."

Norman remained quiet for a minute or two. "Are you saying you know something about these?"

"Make your hair curl," shouted Frankie.

"The robberies?" repeated Norman.

Frankie nodded.

"Have you told the police?" asked Norman.

"Police?" repeated Frankie, shifting his eyes all over the bar and lifting his eyebrows so much they almost disappeared under his hat. "No police, not me. Mouth shut."

"Let me get you another drink, my friend," said Norman.

Chapter Thirty-five

Gardener and Reilly were discussing their next step when Sharp and Rawson slipped into the office. Rawson was carrying three coffees in a cardboard tray, and a bottle of water. Sharp had a bag of sausage rolls from a deli in Bursley Bridge.

When they were all seated, Gardener asked how they had fared at the scrapyard, and if they had their Quasimodo banged to rights and ready to interview.

Over snacks and drinks, Sharp explained where Frankie was, and what they had learned from Derrick Mitchell.

"What's your impression of Mitchell?" Gardener asked.

"He seems right enough," said Rawson. "Gave us some info on this Frankie character."

"It's a weird set-up, really," said Sharp. "Mitchell knows little or nothing about that man, where he comes from, whether or not he has family."

"Does he have a driving licence?" asked Reilly. "What with him doing lots of driving?"

"We asked," said Rawson, "but Mitchell admitted he's never asked. It had never really been part of the plan for Frankie to drive."

"Technically," said Gardener, "I suppose we're not really investigating that, but it's something we can pass on if we have him in here and decide to arrest and charge him for Challenger's murder."

"Problem with that," said Reilly, "is we still don't have any real evidence he did it. We have a text to his phone and a muffled conversation with Challenger."

Gardener nodded his agreement. "It's enough."

"You say you have Mitchell's alibis for the days of the robberies?" Gardener asked Sharp.

Sharp nodded. "His and Frankie's, they were both in the yard on those days."

"Okay, can you verify them, please? See if he's telling the truth, and if at all possible, see if there is any CCTV evidence that backs up the fact that he was where he said he was. We should also have the CCTV from the scrapyard on those particular days. It probably won't show everything, but it might be enough."

"What about Frankie?" asked Rawson. "Do you want us to watch the yard?"

"Sounds good in theory," said Gardener. "But we don't really have the manpower to do that. Hopefully, Mitchell will be true to his word and either send Frankie in, or call us and tell us where he is."

Gardener glanced at his watch. It was approaching six.

"What time did you talk to Mitchell?"

"During lunchtime," said Sharp.

"And we haven't heard anything from Frankie?" asked Reilly. "He should have been back by now."

"According to Mitchell," said Rawson, "he's never back when he should be."

"Mitchell's not bothered, though," said Sharp. "He doesn't pay him enough to worry about it. So long as Frankie does what's asked of him, Mitchell leaves him alone."

"Okay," said Gardener. "For now, verify the alibis. If he hasn't been in touch with us by tomorrow morning, Sean and I will go over there – early. We'll rattle him out of his pit and read him the riot act. This case is really starting to bug me. We know someone's dead, but we can't put anyone in the frame, despite knowing at least one of four people could have been responsible."

"Or all of them," offered Reilly.

"I was wondering," said Sharp, "should we have brought Frankie's money in with us?"

Gardener thought about that. "I don't suppose we can, not until we can prove it *is* from the robberies. He could have acquired the money legitimately. However, we can bring him in for a chat because we have a conversation between him and Challenger on the latter's phone. We would have to see if he can explain his way out of it."

"We also have a text," said Reilly.

"Which, according to Mitchell," said Rawson, "is a waste of time. Old Frankie is dyslexic. Why would you send a text to someone who can't read?"

"That figures," said Reilly. "You remember that day we were there? I offered him the paper for the races and he made up some excuse about not having his glasses."

"Still raises the question," said Sharp. "Who sent that text? It might have come from Challenger's phone, but it doesn't mean he sent it."

"I've thought about that," said Gardener. "We know the van passed Appleby's house at three-thirty, followed by a small Suzuki Swift. The Swift then returned, passing

Appleby's house at four-thirty. That is a one-hour window in which someone disposed of Challenger and the van."

"Which suggests someone other than Frankie and Challenger knew what was happening," said Reilly. "And they were lying in wait."

"Whoever it was, they disposed of Challenger, sent Frankie a text from Challenger's phone, and then waited for him to set the van on fire."

"But something obviously went wrong," said Rawson, "because it probably should have been found totally burnt out."

"Suggesting it should have been torched earlier," said Gardener. "Perhaps by the time that was meant to be found, all evidence should have been destroyed."

"We need to know who was in that Suzuki Swift," said Reilly.

"I know this is shutting the gate after the horse has bolted but did we check Challenger's phone for fingerprints?" asked Gardener. "It might be worth checking to see if we did, and if we didn't, for God's sake let's do it now."

"Maybe the van was being driven to the scrapyard," said Reilly. "That's about the only place I can think of."

"Meaning Mitchell *is* involved," said Rawson.

"Possibly," said Gardener. "Mitchell could be innocent. As we've said, Frankie could be using a legitimate business as a front, and Mitchell might not know anything about it. On the other hand, from what we've seen and heard, his house is very substantial. Would the yard be enough to provide for all that?"

"I wouldn't have thought so," said Reilly. "I know scrap metal is good business these days, but it wouldn't surprise me to find it's only one arm of his business."

"There was a hell of a run on scrap metal a few years ago," said Rawson. "It was booming, maybe he made his money during that period."

"But from what we've discovered," said Gardener, "he bought his house before that period. I think we need to add Mitchell into the fold. Take a closer look."

"There was something else that might put Mitchell in the picture," said Sharp.

"What's that?" asked Gardener.

"He has a crusher."

"Yes," said Rawson. "It's right at the back of the yard, near Frankie's wreck of a van."

"That's interesting," said Reilly.

"It promotes another theory," said Gardener. "All the vans could have been bought by him, used for the robberies, and then crushed straight after, hence the reason they have disappeared?"

Reilly nodded. "Who would be any the wiser?"

Chapter Thirty-six

Mitchell was sitting at the desk in his portacabin nursing a long cold coffee when Norman finally entered.

"Christ! What kept you?"

"You never told me how much that little bastard puts away," Norman said.

"Oh, he's a proper fucking sponge."

"He'd had half a dozen pints or more when I got to him."

Mitchell laughed. "How many have you had?"

"One," said Norman. "He was that pissed he didn't notice I wasn't drinking."

Mitchell stood, left his desk, showing Norman to a seat at the table. He poured two fresh coffees from the percolator. He glanced at the clock and saw it was after ten-thirty.

"Where is he now?"

"No idea," said Norman. "Probably sleeping it off in the van somewhere. He left a while ago."

Mitchell passed Norman's coffee over and then sat at the table with his own.

"What did you find out?"

"Frankie didn't say a lot. Most of the information came from the Sardine."

"Who?"

Norman laughed. "You don't know him but he's pretty sound. His name's Brian Walker, he works at the sausage factory in town."

"Works with sausages and is called Sardine, how does that work out?"

"Apparently his wife used to do his pack up: every day, the same thing, sardine sandwiches. Brian was sick of them, so was everyone else. Anyway, one of his mates suggested he tell his wife to give him something different. Brian said he had, but it had made no difference. Sardines were cheap. His mate told him to get rid of the wife. Next day, Brian came in with chicken sandwiches. His mate asked what had happened and Brian said he'd taken his advice."

"Quick work. Where did she go?"

"No idea," said Norman. "She's never been seen since."

"I don't think we'll go any further. So what's Frankie been up to?"

"Frankie himself was cagey," said Norman, "even with a drink inside him. He rattled on about horses, said a bit about the robberies in the town; but as Frankie left, Sardine came in and asked me what I was doing with the village idiot. Anyway, to cut a long story short, Sardine had been in the pub a few weeks back when he overheard Frankie talking to a man called Davey Challenger."

Mitchell had not heard of Challenger. "About what, as if I couldn't guess?"

"It was late; there might have been a lock-in or something. Frankie was shooting his mouth off."

"That figures," said Mitchell, "especially if he'd been drinking. What the hell was he rattling about?"

"From what Sardine overheard, Frankie hated his life," said Norman. "He was sick of taking orders from one Derrick Mitchell, living in a caravan in the scrapyard."

"It's his choice," retorted Mitchell. "He wouldn't even have the caravan if it wasn't for me."

"Frankie reckoned that he took all the risks, and you creamed off all the money, giving him a pittance."

"Cheeky bastard!" said Mitchell. "The only risks he takes are living in that caravan and waking up in a morning. It's me that does all the work. I take all the risks and plan everything. I only involved him because he's handy and I pay him enough to keep his mouth shut."

"Not working though, Derrick," said Norman. "Anyway, according to Sardine, Frankie was thick in with Challenger, who listened intently. Frankie said that you and he were behind the recent post office jobs. After a few more pints and a bit more buttering up, this Challenger bloke coerced Frankie into helping *him*, promising him a much better cut, leaving you out altogether. He persuaded Frankie that he could pull it off easily because *he* worked for the post office."

"And how the hell were they going to do that?"

"Seems they met a couple of times, in the same place, which happened to be Sardine's local, so he was in prime position to hear everything. They planned to use an old van of yours."

"Mine?" said Mitchell. "But I crush them after they've been used. We do the robbery, bring them back here and crush them straight away."

"Didn't happen with the last van, apparently," said Norman. "Instead of crushing that last Transit, Frankie drove it out of the yard and hid it in a barn ready for another job, which earned him a few pounds. Challenger told Frankie that every possible means of identification had to be removed once the job had been done, before it was torched, so it couldn't be identified."

"And Frankie knows his way around vehicles, so it wouldn't have been too much of a problem," said Mitchell.

"So, the plan was," continued Norman, "you and Frankie would do what you always do, but Challenger would muscle in at the last minute. He would take the money. Once the heat died down, Challenger would drive the van into the field for Frankie to torch and, finally, arrange to meet him and give him his share."

"Double-crossing bastard," said Mitchell. "I don't believe this. It must have been Challenger who took a shot at me, in the post office."

"Sounds like it."

"And he must have shot the postmaster for some reason. That bloke was still standing when we ran out of the shop." Mitchell took a sip of coffee, seething, wondering what to do about it all, then he said, "I've never even heard of Challenger. Who the hell is he?"

"Worked for the post office," said Norman.

"So he's no big time gangster, then," replied Mitchell, "just some small time chancer who thought he'd push his luck."

"Sounds like it," said Norman.

"What do you know about him?"

"Not the sharpest tool in the box, by all accounts. Lived in Bursley Bridge with a bit of a fashion model wife but had some rough bit on the side in Bramfield."

"Wife who looks like a model, and a bit on the side who looks like a wrestler?" said Mitchell. "You're right, he is a sandwich short of a picnic. But then, so is Frankie."

"Frankie's more than one sandwich short."

Mitchell finished his coffee. "Well done, Norman, I'll sort you a chunk out for this. Anyway, I want to know all about this Challenger bloke, whatever you can find, and then I want *him* found and brought here, to me."

"I'd like to help you with that one, Derrick. I can certainly find out about his wife and his mistress. After all someone must have the money. But I'm afraid Challenger is dead."

"Dead?" repeated Mitchell. "What happened to him?"

"He was the body in the van that got set on fire, which is why the police are asking so many questions."

"How the hell did he end up in there? Who put him there?"

"That much I don't know."

"This is ridiculous," said Mitchell. "Them two double-cross me and one of them is then found dead, in the van used in the previous robbery that should have been crushed. What's going on? No wonder the police have been sniffing around, asking questions about the fire and Frankie. I've no idea who the hell is responsible for the fire, or for killing Challenger, but I can't believe Frankie had the bottle, or the intelligence to do it."

Norman leaned forward. "I don't know how true it is, but I've heard that Frankie's fingering you for the fire. He thinks you found out about Challenger, killed him, and then set fire to the van."

"Is he serious?" asked Mitchell.

"Maybe he thinks you're coming for him as well," said Norman. "So he's put the first stake in the ground."

"I don't kill people, Norman. I'll admit that I've often been on the wrong side of the law, done plenty of dodgy deals and I've robbed a few post offices in my time, but I do not kill people. I take risks, and you know why I have to do that, but killing people is a risk too far and definitely not my style."

"Just telling you what I know and what I've heard, Derrick," said Norman, rising. "You may need to lie low for a while, till all this dies down."

"How? If I've been fingered for torching the van and killing someone, it won't be long before the police are questioning me," said Mitchell. "And of that, I'm innocent, but they *will* probe further into it – you know what they're like. Eventually, it'll come out that I've done the robberies, but how the hell do I prove I didn't kill Challenger and set fire to the van? And what happens to me when it comes to the robberies? If I go down, it could have grave consequences."

"If the fire is nothing to do with you, Derrick, find the man who *is* responsible," said Norman, edging toward the open door. "Anyway, you know where I am. I will find out more about the wife and the girlfriend, but if you want my opinion, you'll have a word with that loose cannon of yours. He knows more about this than he's letting on, and I don't think it will take too much to get him to talk, especially if he thinks he's going down for something he didn't do. I'll leave that in your capable hands."

After Norman had left, Mitchell returned to his desk and fired up the CCTV footage from the night of the fire. He studied it closely, three times, but saw nothing.

There was however a camera angle he had not checked, nor had he shown the police when they came sniffing around. Mitchell had another camera behind Frankie's van. Within minutes he saw that Frankie had left his caravan in the early hours of the morning through the hinged side window. There was only one reason he could have done that. *He* must have torched the van. But did he kill Challenger?

Mitchell leaned back, thinking of another question. Who had the money: Frankie, the wife, or the girlfriend?

He also had his brother Terry to consider.

Chapter Thirty-seven

Gardener was sitting in the kitchen a little after three o'clock in the morning, unable to sleep. He'd made himself herbal tea and was trying to work through the case, in some kind of logical order.

The last person he expected to see was his father.

"What are you doing up?" Gardener asked.

"I was just about to ask you the same thing."

"Couldn't sleep."

"Me neither," said Malcolm. "What is your excuse?"

"The case. Yours?"

"My age," said Malcolm. "That's about all I can put it down to. You don't need as much sleep when you're older."

Malcolm used the recently boiled kettle to make a drink before sitting at the table.

"When I was younger, and it happened now and again, I would desperately try anything to get back to sleep. But now, I'm well past my prime, so I have nothing to lose by coming down here and making a brew."

"You probably had nothing to lose then."

"Apart from a day's work. You of all people know how hard it is to work when you're tired."

Malcolm sipped his tea, stood up and reached into a cupboard and dragged out a tin of biscuits.

"Something else you do when you get to my age, you don't worry about calories anymore. So how bad is this case?"

"It's not strictly a bad one, just very puzzling," said Gardener.

"More than one suspect?"

"Four," said Gardener. "But if they're all involved, I haven't found enough evidence to support that theory."

"Nice," said Malcolm, dunking a biscuit. "Tell me about it, maybe I can help."

"I'm not supposed to."

"Never stopped you before."

Gardener laughed. They had spoken on many occasions. He knew the details would never go any further, and it quite often helped to talk it through.

Gardener filled him in on the details. Once he'd finished, he made fresh tea for them both.

Malcolm disappeared into the living room and returned with three different books. That was something he had always admired about his father: he was gardener by name and nature, having owned his own landscaping business for years. He pretty much knew everything there was to know about plants.

Malcolm sat and took a sip of tea. "I know a bit about this stuff."

"Aconitine?"

Malcolm nodded.

"Dangerous stuff, but believe it or not, it's easy enough to extract that from the plant, monkshood. Monkshood is also called wolfsbane. It's a perennial herb, usually grown as an ornamental plant – mainly because the blue to dark purple flowers are very attractive. But all parts of the plant, especially the roots, contain toxins. Aconitine is only one of them. It is a poison that primarily effects the heart but is also a potent nerve poison.

"The raw plant is very poisonous. It can be used as a herb but only after processing by boiling or steaming, which reduces the toxicity."

"Is it widely grown here, in the UK?"

"Oh, yes," said Malcolm.

"Can you show me what it looks like?"

Malcolm did as he was asked. In fact, he found pictures of the plant from all three books.

"One thing is certain," said Malcolm. "You don't need to be an expert to poison yourself, but you do have to be if you want to poison someone else."

Gardener instantly knew where he had seen that plant before.

Chapter Thirty-eight

Frankie woke up with an earth-moving start. He couldn't remember the last time that had happened. He was groggy and felt like shit. The whole bastard room was swimming. What the hell had he drunk last night – and how much?

In fact, he'd actually fallen out of bed, and he couldn't remember the last time that had happened either.

The caravan suddenly lurched to the left and Frankie rolled over, into a cupboard, cracking his head. His pillow fell on top of him. Pity it wasn't there before he hit the fucking cupboard. The whole thing lurched to the right and Frankie rolled back into the side of his bed.

"Jesus Christ," said Frankie, "give us a break, God." He hadn't felt this bad for as long as he could remember.

As he struggled to raise himself, there was a creak and a groan and the van dipped forward, sending Frankie rolling toward the bay window. There was definitely something amiss because hangovers should only be *inside* your head; you don't physically move.

The rear of the van dipped and although Frankie had managed to make it to his knees, the next thing he saw coming toward him was the toilet – and they never moved in hangovers either.

Frankie curled up like a hedgehog and tried to jam himself against a cupboard. As he waited, the movement began to subside and all he was left with was a gentle rocking motion.

He lifted his head from underneath his arms and glanced around, wondering if the Russians had invaded. Nothing else had moved, or was currently moving.

Frankie slowly rose to his knees, grabbed the handle of a drawer and pulled himself upwards. Allowing another half minute to pass, he finally opened the caravan door.

He glanced out and almost shat a paving slab, never mind a brick. The van was suspended at least twenty feet in the air from a mobile crane and was now hovering precariously over the crusher.

Frankie closed his eyes, rubbed them vigorously before reopening them. Nothing was any different. He quickly grabbed a rail at the side of the cupboard and held on for grim death.

Which was when he noticed Derrick Mitchell standing underneath.

"What are you doing?" shouted Frankie.

"I could ask you the same," said Mitchell.

"You're not making sense," said Frankie.

"Since when have you?" asked Mitchell.

Frankie stepped back into the van a little, not that it gave him any more confidence. If he fell out he would ricochet around the yard like a pinball.

"Is there something wrong?" asked Frankie.

Mitchell climbed the crane so he was a little nearer. "Who is Davey Challenger?"

"Who?" said Frankie, nearly shitting himself again, playing for time.

Mitchell pointed. "Don't mess me about. Last time, who is Davey Challenger?"

"I don't know anyone called Challenger." Which wasn't strictly a lie because Challenger was dead.

"You lying little freak," shouted Mitchell. "Look, I'm not going to stand around here all day waiting for you to tell me the truth, so I'll save us all some time and I'll tell *you* what happened with the last robbery, shall I?"

Frankie didn't reply. There was a time and place and now wasn't it.

"I know Davey Challenger was our mystery guest. I know who told him all about the robbery, who sold him a shotgun, and I know that the van from the third robbery was not crushed. What do you have to say about that?"

"Mr Mitchell…"

"Mr Mitchell now, is it?"

"Look, someone's telling you lies."

"That would be you, then," said Mitchell.

Frankie stopped in his tracks. "Well, whoever it is, they've got it wrong."

"Wrong?" said Mitchell. "Are you saying it wasn't Davey Challenger who took a shot at me in the post office?"

Frankie glanced around the yard, but there simply was no escape from his current predicament.

Mitchell continued. "Are you saying it wasn't Davey Challenger who made off with our money, and who agreed to give you a much bigger cut than I ever did?"

Frankie's insides were rumbling.

"Cat got your tongue?" asked Mitchell. "Doesn't matter, Frankie, because I've had enough of this. I've had enough of you. I've looked after you over the years."

"I know you have, Mr Mitchell," pleaded Frankie, hoping his boss was calming down.

"But not anymore. Your deceit could lead everyone to my door. You told Challenger what we were up to. Why, I've no idea. But he decided he wanted some of the action. He has a wife and a mistress, so it's my guess that they also know – or at least one of them will. I can't have loose lips.

I can't have too many people knowing my business. Thanks to you, a lot of people do. And I am going to have to sort these people out, if it's not too late."

"What are you going to do?" Frankie asked.

"Well, Challenger is dead, taken care of, but you'd know all about that, wouldn't you?"

"It was an accident."

"What was?" asked Mitchell. "The van fire, or you spilling your guts?"

"The van fire. I didn't mean to kill anyone." Frankie was blubbering.

"Maybe you didn't, but if you'd kept your trap shut in the first place, none of this would have happened. We wouldn't be having this conversation. But, oh no, what we had wasn't enough. Now, it appears that I'm in the frame for everything, and the only person who could have set me up, is you."

"Who told you that?"

"Is it true?" shouted Mitchell, ignoring Frankie's question.

Tears rolled down Frankie's face. He knew exactly what kind of trouble he was in now and he had no idea how to limit the damage.

"I take it your lack of an answer means it is."

Frankie dropped to his knees. "I'm sorry, Mr Mitchell. I didn't mean for any of this to happen. What are you going to do?"

"There's only one thing I can do, Frankie. I can't keep people I can't trust."

Frankie's insides erupted. "What does that mean?"

"It means," said Mitchell, "that the death count needs to be a little higher. I know what you've done. Instead of crushing the vehicle from the third robbery like you were supposed to, you greedy little shit, you sold it to a man called Davey Challenger, along with a sawn-off 20-bore shotgun with the serial number ground off, for £200. I believe you then drove it out of the yard and hid it in a barn, ready for another job. You were supposed to remove every possible means of identification on that vehicle once that job had been done, and then torch it so nothing would come back to you, or, more importantly, me."

"Mr Mitchell," blubbered Frankie. "I never killed Challenger. I never killed anyone."

"I'm not bothered whether you did or you didn't," said Mitchell. "What bothers me is that you're telling the police that *I* did."

"I never even saw him on the morning involved," shouted Frankie. "I've never killed anyone. I just got this message from him…"

"Message?" shouted Mitchell. "You got a message. What was the fucking point of sending *you* a message, you can't read. How did you know it was from Challenger?"

"It can't have been anyone else," argued Frankie.

"What time did you receive that message?"

"Time?" repeated Frankie.

"Yes, you fucking idiot, what time?"

"I don't know," squealed Frankie.

Mitchell suddenly produced a shotgun. "Tell me what time or I'll blow you fucking head off here and now. And if I miss you with the first, I'll keep blowing holes in that fucking wreck of a van until you fall through the bottom."

Frankie slumped and farted and nearly fell out of the van anyway. He put his hands on the frame of the caravan door.

"I think it was about four o'clock."

"Four o'clock?" shouted Mitchell. "How come you didn't roll out of the yard until two hours later?"

"How do you know that?" pleaded Frankie.

"Answer the fucking question," shouted Mitchell, taking aim.

Frankie shook like a palm tree in a hurricane. "I woke up late, didn't hear the text."

"Precisely," said Mitchell. "That's what caused the problem. What the fuck were you playing at? You being a lazy, greedy little bastard has put everyone in jeopardy – especially Terry. You fat, incompetent freak. Had you got up at the right time, the whole thing could have been burnt out and identification might have been next to impossible. The police are sniffing around and now they suspect everyone. I had nothing to do with that van fire. You know very well that I was only involved in the robberies, and why I was doing it. And because of your incompetence you have managed to fuck it all up for me."

Frankie was on his knees, all snot and tears, snivelling. "I'm sorry. I didn't mean for this to happen."

"At last," shouted Mitchell, lowering the gun. "We finally have an admission." He stepped back toward the crane.

"I'm so sorry, Mr Mitchell," shouted Frankie. "When you let me down from here, I'll make it up to you. I'll never do anything like this again."

"Let you down?" called Mitchell, from the cab of the crane. "Who said I'm letting you down?"

Frankie quickly stood up, his jeans stained back and front. "What are you going to do?"

Mitchell shut the cab door, started the crane and operated the levers. Quickly, he drew the caravan over the opening of the crusher.

"No," shouted Frankie. "Mr Mitchell, what are you doing?"

Frankie watched in shock horror as his caravan plummeted, into the crusher. He almost fell out, wished he had, but now the sides of the crusher were blocking his exit.

The crane motor stopped.

The crusher motor fired into life.

The walls started to move inwards.

Frankie started to scream.

Chapter Thirty-nine

Gardener was in the incident room early. Following the conversation with his father in the early hours, sleep had continued to evade him, so he had taken himself into the garage to polish the Triumph, whilst listening to some background music, all of which allowed him some thinking time.

The team filed in and took their seats. Cragg slipped in behind them. Before the meeting started, Cragg told Gardener that something had happened late last night he felt the team ought to know about.

Gardener nodded.

"I took an anonymous call. Someone was desperate to tell us that he had information about the post office robberies. He reckoned Derrick Mitchell was responsible for the robberies, and that Mitchell also killed Challenger, and torched the van. He said Mitchell was a dangerous man and we needed to take a closer look at him."

"Did this person have any proof?" asked Gardener.

"I asked him, but he didn't want to stay on the line too long," said Cragg. "In case we traced it, he reckoned. And apparently, he was frightened for his own safety."

"Did you recognise the caller?" Gardener asked Cragg.

Cragg nodded. "I certainly did. It was Frankie, Mitchell's sidekick."

"Was it now?" said Reilly. "So what's he up to? Why is he throwing his boss under a bus?"

"Did he mention the other person involved in the last robbery?" Gardener asked.

"No, only Mitchell."

"And he also reckons that Mitchell killed Challenger as well?" said Reilly.

Cragg nodded.

"If Mitchell is responsible for the post office robberies," said Gardener, "then he would certainly have a motive for killing Challenger after what happened with the last one."

"Especially as Challenger made it off with the money," said Anderson.

"Why has Frankie suddenly decided to tell us this?" asked Thornton. "And why didn't he tell us who the other person was?"

"Unless the other person was Frankie himself," offered Cragg.

"Not according to Mitchell," said Rawson. "No one would employ that clown."

"He does," said Reilly. "It's not too much of a stretch to think that a man like Mitchell would keep a close reign on Frankie. He makes out that Frankie is stupid and no one would employ him, but maybe he isn't. If Mitchell is involved in the robberies, then he's probably using Frankie."

"A lot of people are implying a lot of things at the moment," said Gardener. "I think it's time we found out who knows what and, if necessary, we'll turn up the heat by bringing everyone in. We'll arrest and interview everybody. That should sort out the men from the boys. But firstly, who has information to share with us?"

Sharp finally had CCTV footage from the Shell station in Birmingham.

"At last," said Gardener. "What does it show?"

Sharp slotted the USB stick into the laptop on the desk, which in turn fed the images through to the overhead projector. The camera picked up Mitchell's low-loader, with two vehicles firmly fastened on to it. Because of that, you couldn't quite see who was filling a jerrycan, until he went to pay for it. Inside, at the counter, Frankie paid for the fuel, and a shedload of food.

"Well," said Gardener. "That's him nailed. What that footage suggests to me is, everything has been well planned. Frankie knows what he is doing because he's not been stupid enough to buy the fuel locally. He's taken the opportunity to use an out-of-town trip so as not to be noticed.

"The question now is," continued Gardener, "is Frankie stupid, or is it all an act? Does he make himself look stupid to others so they will leave him alone? We've seen him a couple of times and on both occasions you can't make head nor tail of what the hell he's talking about, but is that what he wants?"

"Either way," said Reilly, "this hasn't helped him."

Gardener turned to Gates and Longstaff. "Can we have another look at the CCTV footage of the robberies? Until now, we've paid little attention to the first two men involved because everything happened quickly, and they were wearing masks and gloves. But Frankie's shape is not so easy to disguise."

The girls spent a few minutes sorting through it, and then played everything back. The footage from the first robbery in Thirsk did not clearly put Frankie in the picture. The man they suspected might be him spent most of the time behind shelves. The same thing happened in Thornton le Dale, robbery number two. But number three was a different story. The CCTV inside the shop offered a better view. The robber who collected the shopkeeper's mobile was rather a large man. Despite the mask, Gardener felt confident the man was a match with Frankie.

"That's good enough for me," said Gardener. "We'll have him in and we'll find out what he's involved in and whether or not he really is as stupid as he makes out."

Gardener put a tick against Frankie's name on the whiteboard then questioned Longstaff and Gates again.

"Anything on the van?"

"Yes," said Gates. "After trawling the local CCTV in the town we've discovered that on the day of the fourth robbery, Davey Challenger parked the van in a layby on Undercliffe, not far from the railway station. The footage then shows him leaving the van, walking in the direction of the town."

"Didn't happen to have a gun with him, did he?" asked Gardener.

"No," said Gates. "He obviously had it hidden somewhere on route."

Gardener nodded, allowing them to continue.

"Later that night when he returned to retrieve the van," said Longstaff, "CCTV picked him up."

"What time did he return to the van?" asked Gardener.

"Late," said Gates, checking her notes. "Early hours of the morning, two forty-five."

"His wife states that he left the house around seven-thirty," said Gardener. "He told her he was playing darts, but there was no darts match. He can't have been with Monica because she was working the night shift, so where the hell had he been for all that time? Anyway, not that it matters now. Was the van picked up by CCTV anywhere else after he'd collected it?"

"Only once, leaving the town and heading towards Bramfield," said Gates.

"Although we can't tell exactly where he went with it," said Longstaff. "The road to Bramfield would have taken him past Haygate Lane."

Gardener nodded. "Which is where Appleby's CCTV recorded him."

"There is more," said Gates.

Gardener grabbed his bottled water and took a drink before asking them to continue.

"The very same CCTV that picked up Challenger and his van in the town," said Gates, "also picked up the same small purple car that we've all been trying to identify."

"Where?" asked Gardener.

"Where he collected the van, on Undercliffe," said Longstaff. "A minute or so after he'd set off, the car was following. It was still following him when he left town, heading towards Bramfield."

"And we know it was still following him on Haygate Lane, so I'm inclined to believe that it was no coincidence," offered Gardener. "Question is, have we managed to see the registration?"

"Yes," said Gates. "The car belongs to Grace Challenger."

"Are we able to see the driver?" asked Gardener.

"Not yet," said Longstaff. "The tech boys are on it and I'm hoping we can have something before we finish here."

"Even if we don't," said Gardener, "it's too much of a stretch to think someone else was driving Grace's car at three o'clock in the morning, following the van that was eventually torched with her husband's body inside."

"Which puts Grace Challenger in the frame," said Reilly. "Not only for the death of her husband, but possibly torching the van as well."

"I'm still not sure about her torching the van, Sean," said Gardener. "The murder… possibly? She had enough time. The van is picked up at two forty-five. It's next seen a short while later, leaving the town, then on Haygate Lane at three-thirty. Each time it's seen, the small purple car is following. The next time we see anything is four-thirty, when the small purple car returns back past Appleby's house – but no van.

"By that time," continued Gardener. "Grace has probably caught up with her husband, poisoned him, rendered him disabled, and managed to get him into the van, possibly driven it into the field and left it for someone else to torch."

"Which has to be Frankie," said Longstaff. "Because it's his phone that received the text saying, 'all yours'."

"Which Grace must have sent from her husband's phone," said Gardener. "Meaning she's also been lying all along, especially about the phone. She said that she didn't know where it was, and then she told us she had found it in the garage."

"What I can't understand," said Sharp, "is why Grace would get into bed with Frankie. Those two are polar opposites."

"Maybe she didn't," said Gardener. "If she's followed everything that her husband has been up to, and plotted everything out very carefully, maybe she only had to send that one text. After all, as far as Frankie was concerned, that text came from Challenger himself."

He turned to Gates and Longstaff. "When we've finished here, can you contact her nearest neighbours to see if any of them noticed her using the car on the night in question?"

Gardener's phone suddenly chimed. A quick conversation followed, after which, he informed the team that the call had been from the head of CSI, Steve Fenton, confirming that they did turn Grace Challenger's house upside down on the day they searched the place, including the garage. There was no phone.

"That's her nailed," said Gardener. "And during the early hours of this morning, I came across something else that, for me, probably puts the final nail in her coffin."

Chapter Forty

"In the early hours?" questioned Cragg.

Gardener nodded. "Long story, Maurice."

The door opened and Tom Wilkinson stepped in. "Sorry I'm late."

Reilly glanced at his watch and then back at Wilkinson.

"I know you're dedicated, old son, but you can't have been at the cakes already."

"No," said Wilkinson with a smile. "I had to drop the grandchildren off at school. Their mother has some kind of Zoom meeting."

"So you haven't made it to the café?" asked Reilly, his stomach rumbling on cue.

Wilkinson shook his head. "No, thought I might head that way after here."

Gardener allowed him a few minutes to settle himself, and then brought Wilkinson up to date on what they had discussed.

"Which leads me nicely to the early hours of this morning," said Gardener. "I couldn't sleep, neither could my father. We both ended up downstairs, drinking tea and chatting about the case. As most of you know, he is a bit of an encyclopaedia when it comes to gardens and herbs and plants. We talked about it, and he told me something interesting about aconitine, stressing how dangerous it is, and how you can extract it *if* you have enough knowledge."

Gardener grabbed his phone, connected it to the laptop and downloaded the pictures his father had shown him.

"What are we supposed to be looking at?" asked Longstaff.

"Those blue and purple flowers are monkshood," said Gardener, pointing. "We all know someone who has a very cultured garden and knows a lot about herbs and plants – including these things, I wouldn't mind betting."

"Grace Challenger," said Reilly.

"Precisely," said Gardener. "Every time we go to her house, she has a tray of freshly picked flowers and veg."

Gardener went on to explain the extraction process his father had mentioned.

"Grace Challenger is the one person who has been hiding in plain sight. I honestly believe that she is responsible for her husband's death. She had the time to carefully work her way through it. Ever since she found out about his affair, she has been on to him. If you look at the way she runs her life, she does it with extreme precision. What's to say she'd done this any different? She plotted her revenge, followed him; probably checked his phones and very possibly his other computer equipment on a regular basis, before striking at precisely the right time. Furthermore, she has been clever enough to implicate other people."

"But she isn't responsible for the robberies," said Wilkinson.

"True," said Gardener. "The likelihood is, those are down to Mitchell. But I don't think *he* killed Challenger. If Mitchell did kill Challenger, where would he have obtained the poison? I believe that's just Frankie shooting his mouth off for whatever reason because he's in some kind of trouble with Mitchell, and he's trying to get the first shot in."

"Unless he's in league with Grace Challenger," said Reilly.

"It's more likely to be Mitchell who's in league with Grace, not Frankie," said Rawson.

"We're pretty certain Grace poisoned her husband," said Benson, "but there's still the question of how?"

"Maybe she's slowly been slipping it into his food over a period of time," suggested Thornton.

"Wouldn't be the first time that method has been employed," said Gates.

"If anyone were capable of doing it through food, it would be Grace," said Gardener. "I suspect she cooked and controlled all the meals. But I'm still not sure she did it that way. I think that would take far too long, possibly cause side effects that she couldn't control, and might well disable him before the job was done. What happened here suggests something much quicker."

"A syringe?" suggested Reilly.

"That's exactly what I was thinking," said Gardener, turning to Cragg. "Maurice, will you do me a small favour? Can you call Monica Rushby, to ask her if she keeps any medical equipment at the house – does she have a good stock of everything, including syringes?"

Cragg nodded and left the room.

"Grace has tried to implicate Monica Rushby in all of this, but she's had solid alibis," Gardener continued, "which is probably the one thing Grace has overlooked. We know the two of them have been friendly, and Grace has been to Monica's house on more than one occasion. We know Grace knows about Monica's condition because that is how they first met. I think Grace Challenger has very carefully plotted how to deal with this situation, and I wouldn't mind betting she has used Monica's condition, and her occupation to try to pin everything on to her."

Cragg returned to the room. "Well done, sir. Monica Rushby keeps a very good stock of medical supplies at her house, including syringes. Being a nurse, she keeps careful control over them, and she believes – although she can't prove it – that some of her syringes are missing."

Gardener nodded and put a tick against Grace Challenger's name on the whiteboard.

"There is something else, sir," said Cragg. "I've just taken a call about George Spencer, the postmaster."

"It's not good news, is it?" asked Gardener.

"No," said Cragg. "Sorry, but he's passed away."

"Oh dear," said Gardener. After a pause he continued. "Okay, this is how it looks to me. Mitchell and Frankie are responsible for the post officer robberies. I have no idea why they would do it, but we'll find that out soon enough because I want them in here as soon as possible. I believe that Grace Challenger killed her husband and dumped him in the van, but I don't believe she set fire to it."

Gardener turned to Gates and Longstaff. "Can you two ladies go and bring in Grace, please? And I'd also like her garden inspecting for the monkshood."

"This is the bit I like," said Anderson. "Finding out who's responsible and dragging them all in and applying a bit of heat."

"I take it we're leaving Monica Rushby out of all this?" asked Cragg.

Gardener nodded. "I don't believe that Monica is involved at all. She is simply a pawn in a dangerous game, and I'd prefer to leave her where she is for now."

"That just leaves those two at the yard," said Reilly.

"That one is a little trickier," said Gardener.

He turned and asked Sharp and Rawson to join him and Reilly to bring in Mitchell and Frankie.

"Would you like to join us on that one, Tom?" asked Gardener. "It is your case."

Tom Wilkinson nodded. "But I have to admit, I'm not one for violence."

"Don't worry about that," said Rawson. "We have him with us." He pointed to Reilly. "And as you well know, we haven't fed him yet."

Chapter Forty-one

Around fifty yards from the end of East Ings Lane, the entrance to the scrapyard, Gardener asked the young PC who was driving, to stop the car. He turned to Reilly.

"Sean, can you jump out here and have a scout around the rear of the place? If Frankie is outside and sees any of this, he's wily enough to have an escape route through the back somewhere. I don't want to leave here without anyone this time."

Reilly nodded, jumping out, leaving Gardener and Wilkinson in the lead car, with Sharp and Rawson in the one behind.

"Are you ready?" asked Gardener.

"As I'll ever be," said Wilkinson.

Both cars set off and pulled into the yard within seconds. Gardener jumped out, surveyed the area, disappointed not to see anyone. Everything appeared normal. The door to the portacabin was open.

Gardener walked over and stepped inside. Mitchell's computer was on, the monitor displaying a 3D-pipes screensaver pattern. A radio on a ledge provided background music. Gardener stepped over to the coffee percolator. It was hot, suggesting that wherever Mitchell was, he wasn't far away.

Gardener stepped back out. All three officers were waiting.

"No one home?" asked Rawson.

"No, but he'll be around here somewhere," replied Gardener. "Everything in there is switched on and the coffee is hot."

"Shall we split up?" asked Sharp.

"Might be a good idea. You and Dave go to the left, and Tom and I will take this side. No heroics, we're not really sure what this man is capable of."

"I shouldn't worry too much," said Rawson. "You've already let the Rottweiler out on his own."

Gardener smiled at his partner's reputation.

Sharp and Rawson set off and Gardener motioned for Wilkinson to follow him.

"Do you think he might be armed?" Wilkinson asked Gardener.

"I'm hoping not," replied the SIO. "It's not as if he's expecting us."

"I suppose it might all depend on whether or not he's found out about Frankie grassing him up."

"Nothing would surprise me," said Gardener, passing a column of cars and slipping down a small corridor to his left, eyes all over the place. "I can't imagine there's much that goes on without Mitchell knowing; he just seems that kind of character."

Gardener stopped and cocked his head to one side, surprised that he couldn't hear anything. He was in a scrapyard. He would have expected something, a drill or a saw going off somewhere, a clanking of spanners, even the odd conversation carried by the breeze. But the place was silent.

As he was about to move, Gardener thought he heard a voice, coming from his right. He bent down and waved his arm for Wilkinson to do the same. As he waited, no other sound came, leading him to believe he might have imagined it.

However, as he rounded the next tower of cars, he instantly knew he *had* heard a voice.

It had been Mitchell's, who was leaning back against a huge oil drum, in front of a pile of cars, three high.

And he was armed.

Although the gun was lowered toward the ground, not held high in a threatening manner, it had been enough to stop Rawson and Sharp from pursuing the matter.

"Come and join us," said Mitchell.

Gardener walked a little closer in. "Mr Mitchell, we'd like to ask you some questions down at the station."

"And it took four of you to tell me that?"

"You can hardly blame us for that," said Gardener. "We have evidence implicating you in a series of armed robberies. It's very unlikely we would send a police constable to come and get you. And here we are, proved right."

"Armed robberies?" asked Mitchell. "I wonder where you dug up that little bit of information."

"If you could just put the gun down, Mr Mitchell and come with us, maybe we can clear all this up."

"Is it just the armed robberies you want to talk to me about, or are you also trying to fit me up for murder?"

"Like I said, if you'll just lower the gun and come along quietly, we can discuss everything back at the station."

Suddenly, Mitchell stepped forward and did the opposite. Instead of lowering the gun, he raised it.

"I want it known here and now, I did not kill Challenger and I did not torch that van."

Everyone took a step back.

"Please put the gun down, Mr Mitchell. I won't ask you again."

"Why? What are you going to do? None of you are armed, which puts me in charge. And unless you listen to me now, and note what I have to say, we are going nowhere."

Gardener was about to speak when Reilly suddenly appeared at the top of the pile of three cars that Mitchell was standing in front of. His heart sunk. He knew his partner was completely unpredictable and anything could happen right now.

He realized the other officers had also seen him, but no one gave his position away by staring up at the cars.

"Come on, Derrick," said Rawson, moving a step closer. "This is not going to help your case."

Mitchell swung the gun to his right.

"You must realize the game is up. You're not going to use that thing, and even if you do, you'll only shoot one of us before the rest of us have you."

"Brave words," said Mitchell.

"It's probably not even loaded."

Mitchell stepped away from the barrel. "Would you like to find out?"

Reilly decided that that was the exact moment to take flight from the top of the pile of cars. The first Mitchell knew was when Reilly's closed fists cracked the back of his head. Mitchell went down like a sack of spuds. Reilly landed on top of him. The gun flew to the right, and it did go off, the cartridge taking out the windscreen of a car three feet right of Rawson.

"Fuck," shouted Rawson, bent double, with his head in his hands.

Sharp was standing in exactly the same position he had been the whole time, but his face was a little paler.

Gardener immediately sprinted over to Mitchell, who was now being hauled up with his hands behind his back. Gardener produced a pair of handcuffs and slipped them around Mitchell's wrists.

He turned to his partner. "There's something not right with you."

"You always say the nicest things."

"That could have gone so wrong."

"No one was going anywhere," said Reilly. "It could have lasted for days."

Gardener smiled. "It is appreciated."

He then turned to Mitchell and read him his rights.

"Did you find Frankie?" Gardener asked Reilly.

"No. He's not there, and neither is his caravan."

"His caravan's gone?" questioned Gardener. "What's happened? It's rotted away to nothing?"

Reilly smirked. "You'd have thought so." He turned to Mitchell as he continued, "But there's a big empty space where it used to be. Do you know anything about that?"

"Why would I?" asked Mitchell.

"He's your employee, Mr Mitchell," said Gardener. "So where is he?"

"I have no idea. Frankie is a law unto himself. I'm not his mother."

Gardener addressed Reilly and Wilkinson. "Can you two escort him back to the car, please?"

Both men took Mitchell away.

Gardener turned to Sharp and Rawson. "Are you two okay?"

"We'll live," said Rawson.

"That was a rather brave move to take," said Gardener to Rawson.

"I was trying to keep Mitchell from seeing the Terminator," said Rawson. "He was the brave one, not me."

"It's much appreciated," said Gardener. "I'm going back to the station with Mitchell, we'll get him signed in and interview him, but I'm not happy with Frankie's disappearance."

"You think something serious might have happened?" said Sharp. "Especially as the caravan is missing."

"I think so," said Gardener. "And I'd lay odds that Mitchell is behind it, so would you two have a good look around the yard? See if you come across anything out of the ordinary?"

"Will do," said Rawson. "We'll see you back at the station."

Chapter Forty-two

It was some two hours later before Gardener and Wilkinson were ready to speak to Mitchell. During that time he had written up all the relevant paperwork created by an arrest, and had also overseen Grace's arrival. He'd placed her in a room, fully intending to speak to her with Reilly, once he had heard what Derrick Mitchell had to say.

Gardener and Wilkinson were in Gardener's office, discussing how best to handle it.

"Nice work by your man back there," said Wilkinson to Gardener.

The SIO was amused by the comment. "We never worry about a situation when we have him with us."

"I'll bet you don't. Is he always like that?"

"Life's never boring with him around," said Gardener.

"Well, he did a great job," said Wilkinson. "Now, to the job in hand. There are a couple of ways we can go."

"It's your case, Tom," said Gardener. "I'm happy to let you lead."

"Okay. Well, the way I see it is, a person is guilty of robbery if he steals, and immediately before, or at the time of doing so, and in order to do so, he uses force on any person, or puts or seeks to put any person in fear being then and there, subjected to force. This is against the Theft Act 1968, so we would charge him for each offence."

It all sounded very textbook to Gardener but he nodded his approval. He was with him so far.

"The CPS however," continued Wilkinson, "like to charge as many varied offences as possible, because it has an impact on sentencing. So we have to look at the fact that he was armed with a shotgun on robberies three and four, which means we can also charge firearms offences. We now know a postmaster was killed. And I believe someone was injured, so manslaughter can be added – that kind of thing."

"If we're going down that route," said Gardener. "They had a getaway vehicle so I'm sure we can add dangerous driving."

"You're getting the idea," said Wilkinson. "We know he must have been acting with someone else, even in the planning, so we can look at conspiracy to rob. There really is no end to what we can add here. But often, if you have a large number of offences, and someone *is* coughing for them, we might look at having a number taken into consideration."

"Which means they're not treated as charges for the purpose of sentencing," said Gardener, "but they will sit on his record charge?"

"Yes," said Wilkinson. "So, maybe it's time we went and had a talk with this man. See what he's willing to give up easily – if anything."

Both men left the room and entered the cell to find Mitchell sitting comfortably with a coffee, and the duty solicitor. Gardener had no idea who the solicitor was but he didn't look experienced enough to handle what Mitchell was facing. He couldn't have been more than twenty-five years old, with long mousy brown hair, tortoiseshell glasses, a pockmarked face, and a thin frame. He was wearing jeans, T-shirt and a jacket.

Once seated, and the equipment switched on, Wilkinson went through the usual routine with the recording device.

"Mr Mitchell," said Wilkinson. "You do realize why we want to speak to you today?"

"The armed post office robberies," replied Mitchell.

The solicitor said and did nothing.

"Yes–" said Wilkinson, but that was as much of the sentence as he managed.

"Guilty," said Mitchell.

"Pardon?" said Wilkinson.

"I said, guilty. I am guilty of robbing the post offices."

The solicitor still said and did nothing, which made Gardener wonder if it was Mitchell's plan, and the brief would have to roll with it.

"You're admitting to all four post office robberies?" asked Wilkinson.

"Yes," said Mitchell. "It's going to save everyone a lot of time and energy if I admit my guilt. And my solicitor tells me that I may also be looking at a lighter sentence if I cooperate."

"That's very good of you, Mr Mitchell," said Gardener. "But there is quite a lot to take into consideration here. It's not simply the robberies, but a number of related offences that will come into play: firearms, assault, dangerous driving, etc."

"That's as may be," said Mitchell. "But murder will certainly not be one of them."

"You said back in the yard that you did not kill Davey Challenger, and that you wanted that noting. For the purpose of the tape, are you still maintaining that you did not kill him?" Wilkinson asked.

"Yes," said Mitchell. "I did not kill Challenger. I didn't even know him. I was as surprised as anyone when he muscled in on the last robbery – *and* took off with the money."

"So you were not working *with* Davey Challenger?" Gardener asked.

"I wasn't working with anyone."

"You must have been working with someone," said Wilkinson. "There were always two people present at each robbery. Who was with you?"

"No comment," said Mitchell.

"Why do you want to take the blame for all of this?" asked Wilkinson. "There was quite clearly someone working with you on every robbery. Surely you can give us a name."

Mitchell remained silent.

"Was it Frankie?" asked Gardener.

Mitchell snorted. "That fat clown. Do you honestly think I would use someone so inept?"

"When we first spoke to you," said Gardener, "you told us Frankie was cheap, and he was loyal. You always knew where to find him. It stands to reason it would be Frankie. Now it appears that we seem to have lost Frankie, and I'm still wondering if you know anything about that. So I have to ask you once again, Mr Mitchell, do you know where Frankie is?"

"No comment," said Mitchell.

"Why did you do it?" asked Wilkinson.

Gardener noticed that question had hit a nerve, and Mitchell took an age before he glanced at his solicitor, who only nodded in reply.

"I did it for Terry."

"Terry?" asked Wilkinson. "Who is Terry?"

Mitchell didn't reply.

"Is Terry the other man with you in the post office robberies?" asked Gardener.

Finally, Mitchell said, "He's my brother."

After a brief pause, Wilkinson asked, "Why were you robbing post offices *for* your brother?"

"I owe it to him."

"Owe it?" asked Wilkinson. "Do you mean you borrowed some money from him and you needed a way to pay it back?"

"No," said Mitchell. "But he needs it all the same."

"Instead of us having to guess everything, Mr Mitchell," said Gardener. "Would you like to *tell* us the whole story and save us all a lot of time?"

Eventually, with a desperately haunted expression, Mitchell broke his silence.

"Terry is ill, seriously ill. He is being cared for in a private clinic because he has motor neurone disease."

"I'm sorry," said Gardener. "I'm guessing it must be quite severe if he's in a private clinic."

"Yes," said Mitchell. "It's not a very common condition. It affects the brain and the nerves, which causes a severe weakness that gets worse over time."

"Is there a cure for it?" asked Wilkinson.

"No," said Mitchell. "You can get treatment to help reduce the impact it has on your daily life. Some people live with the condition for years, but it usually does shorten life expectancy, and eventually leads to death."

"How long has he had it?" asked Gardener.

"About eighteen months," said Mitchell. "I found him one day, at the yard. I thought he'd just tripped over something, but as I looked around, I couldn't see anything that could have caused it. I asked him what was wrong, but he just tried to laugh it off. Eventually, a load of other things were happening. He started struggling with stairs –

couldn't climb them. Then he was slurring his speech, as if he were drunk. I thought at first he'd had a stroke but both sides of his body seemed okay.

"And it was all sorts of stupid things that you take for granted. There were times when he couldn't swallow food. He had no strength, couldn't grip anything; couldn't open jars, or do up buttons. He was always dropping things. And then came the big one – weight loss. He started getting thinner. He couldn't disguise that, not from me, anyway. Eventually I said I was taking him to the doctor. He resisted at first, but I was having none of it. That's when we found out."

No one spoke, so Mitchell continued.

"The doctor said it was difficult to diagnose motor neurone disease in the early stages. There was no test for it, and that several conditions could cause similar symptoms. They sent us to a neurologist. He eventually scanned Terry's brain and spine. He ran tests to measure the electrical activity in his muscles and nerves, and he did something called a lumbar puncture. He used a thin needle to remove and test the fluid from within Terry's spine.

"That was it, job done. There was nothing anyone could do. There were a whole range of specialist treatments: highly specialised clinics with occupational therapy to make life easier for him. Certainly didn't make it easier for me. He had to have physiotherapy and lots of exercises to maintain strength and reduce stiffness. He had to take advice from a speech and language therapist, and a dietitian about the right food to eat.

"There were a number of medicines – again, none of them cheap. It just went on and on, and as you can imagine, it literally ate away most of the money we'd had invested."

Mitchell stopped talking then.

"So you thought one obvious solution was to start robbing post offices?" asked Wilkinson.

"I couldn't see him suffer, could I?" said Mitchell. "He was my older brother. He practically brought me up. I bought the house in Morton for us, because he loved it so much. It was Terry who had the vision to turn it into some kind of bird and animal sanctuary. And then all that shit happened, and he's now in a clinic. I needed the money not only to look after him, but to hopefully convert a wing of the house specifically for him, so he could come home."

"Did you think you might get away with it forever?" asked Gardener.

"I knew I wouldn't," said Mitchell. "Only long enough to get what I needed."

Mitchell was pale. His eyes were vacant, and Gardener wondered how he had managed to keep a cool head.

"But I never killed Challenger, nor did I torch the van," insisted Mitchell.

"Can you prove that?" Wilkinson asked.

"Yes," said Mitchell. "I have an alibi for the night of the murder. I was at the clinic with Terry, all night." Mitchell stared Wilkinson in the eye. "Should be easy enough to check."

Which, as far as Gardener was concerned, left Grace or Frankie as the number one suspect; however, it wasn't Frankie who had been following Challenger on the night in question, but it didn't rule him out entirely.

A knock on the door interrupted the meeting. Sharp popped his head around the door and asked Gardener if he could have a word.

Once outside, Gardener asked what was wrong.

"We've found Frankie's caravan."

"Well done," said Gardener. "Where is it, and was he with it?"

"It never left the scrapyard," said Sharp.

"It never left?" questioned Gardener. "Where the hell was it? We never saw it."

"Frankie was definitely with it," said Rawson. "In fact, he was still in it."

"Is this a puzzle?"

"He couldn't possibly get out of it," said Sharp. "It had been through the crusher."

"We could just see the top of his woolly hat," said Rawson, "covered in blood. Looks like someone learned of Frankie's indiscretion and took the matter into his own hands."

Gardener sighed, disappointed. "It can only be our friend in there."

Gardener strolled back into the room and asked Wilkinson to join them outside. All recording was terminated whilst Gardener explained what his team had discovered.

"Looks like this is going to take longer than we thought," said Wilkinson.

Chapter Forty-three

"Why am I here?" asked Grace.

Gardener had read through all the preliminaries for the sake of the recording equipment. Reilly was also in the interview room. Grace had chosen not to contact a solicitor, yet. The only extra piece of equipment was a computer and monitor.

"You're helping with our inquiries," said Gardener.

"And you had to charge me for that, did you?"

"We haven't charged you, Mrs Challenger. My officers were instructed to arrest you and read you your rights."

"Oh, yes, I remember. You arrested me on suspicion of murdering my husband," said Grace. "As if."

Gardener opened the file in front of him, studied the notes, and then placed them back on the table. "You often find it's the little things in life that let you down, don't you think?"

"Couldn't agree more," said Grace.

"Inconsistencies. Loose ends."

"Do get to the point, Inspector," said Grace. "I'd rather not be here all day."

"The first time we met and spoke to you about your husband, you said he had been secretive, quiet, not his usual self. You knew there was something on his mind but during that particular meeting you never said what it might be."

"I didn't know."

"You had no idea of his involvement in the post office robbery at Bursley Bridge?"

"None."

"Let's return to the last night that you actually saw him," said Gardener. "You said you were in all night. Did you at any point, leave the house at all, for anything?"

"I told you I didn't. I was home alone, all evening."

"You say he left the house at seven-thirty for a darts match?"

"That's what he told me," said Grace. "I now know there *was* no darts match."

"And that was the last time you saw your husband? You never saw him again after seven-thirty?"

"No."

"And you still say that you never left the house yourself?" asked Reilly.

"What is this? I've already told you, no."

Gardener made a point of opening the folder and adding notes.

"So, you have no idea where he was during that time?" asked Gardener.

"I could hazard a guess," replied Grace. "Now we all know what he's been up to with another woman."

"The other woman being, Monica Rushby?" said Reilly.

"I'd rather not talk about her, thank you."

"I'm afraid you're going to have to," said Gardener. "How long have you known Monica?"

Grace sighed. "Is all this really necessary?"

"Just answer the question," retorted Reilly.

"About three or four months."

"How did you meet?"

Grace told exactly the same story Monica Rushby had told the two detectives.

"Did you meet often after that first introduction?"

"A few times."

"Where?"

"We met a couple of times in a café."

"Where else?" asked Reilly.

"I went to her house once or twice."

"Did she ever come to yours?"

"Not that I can remember."

"What did you talk about during those meetings?"

"All sorts of things: holidays, television, the state of the country."

"Would you say you shared interests?"

"Yes, we had a lot in common."

"Such as?"

"My husband, for one."

"Is it fair to say that until yesterday, you saw her as a friend?" asked Gardener.

"Yes," replied Grace. "I liked her, and I felt sorry for her, having to live with that condition she has. I even wondered if I had anything in my garden that might help."

"Yet as soon as you found out about the infidelity, you decided she was responsible for your husband's murder. Why?" Gardener asked.

"She's a nurse. She had the knowledge, the opportunity and the equipment to be able to pull it off. Who else could it be?"

"Equipment?" questioned Gardener.

"Yes, equipment," replied Grace. "She worked in a hospital, where better to pick up syringes and the likes?"

"How do you know a syringe was used on your husband?" asked Reilly.

"I don't," replied Grace. "I'm guessing, but I bet I'm not wrong. Stands to reason she is one of the main suspects."

"I take it by 'the likes'," said Gardener. "You mean aconitine?"

"As I said, she worked in a hospital."

Opening the folder and glancing at the top page, Gardener said, "According to you in a previous interview, you thought someone called Frankie had killed your husband."

"Well, it could also have been him," said Grace. "He's a notorious bank robber. Have you spoken to *him* yet?"

"We can understand why Frankie might be involved," said Gardener. "But Monica? I'm having trouble placing her for the killing. Why would she do it?"

"You'll have to ask her," replied Grace.

"We're asking you," said Reilly.

"*Why* are you asking me?" retorted Grace.

"Because you implicated her," said Gardener. "Yet you had little or no proof."

"No proof," shouted Grace. "My husband left everything to her in his will. What if she knew this, and decided she couldn't wait for whatever little treasures he had?"

"Still all guesswork," said Reilly. "You're surmising she knew about the will."

"According to you, he didn't have much," said Gardener. "Most of what you had was down to you. If that had been the case, Monica would be very disappointed now, wouldn't she?"

Grace remained silent.

"Perhaps Monica already knew he didn't have much," said Reilly. "After all, they were having a relationship for quite some time. People usually discuss that type of thing. If she already knew he didn't have anything, she wouldn't be expecting anything, should anything happen to him – therefore, no motive."

"Quite apart from the fact that Monica Rushby has a cast-iron alibi for the night in question," said Gardener.

"She was working," said Reilly. "All night."

Grace stared Reilly in the eye. "You're the detective, you tell me who it was."

"You," said Gardener.

"Pardon?"

"I said, you."

"Don't be ridiculous," said Grace. "Why would I kill my own husband?"

"Maybe because you've known about the affair a lot longer than you make out," offered Reilly.

"And you think I would stand for that, do you? My husband cheating on me for all and sundry to see, and I would stand by and say nothing?"

"You didn't, did you?" asked Gardener.

"Like I said, don't be ridiculous," retorted Grace. "Do you have any proof?"

"As a matter of fact, we do," said Gardener.

Grace blanched.

"As I mentioned, at the start of the interview, it's the little things in life that let you down," said Gardener. "Your garden is one to die for. You have everything in there: herbs, veg, flowers, including one that could do some serious damage if you know what you're doing."

"Which is?" questioned Grace.

"Monkshood."

"A lot of people have monkshood in their gardens, that isn't much in the way of proof."

"Yes, you're right," said Gardener. "Let's go for something a little more solid, then, shall we? What car do you drive, Mrs Challenger?"

"What does that have to do with anything?"

Gardener ignored the question. "Would it be a purple Suzuki Swift, by any chance?" He also read out her registration.

Grace didn't answer.

"I take it by your silence that you do."

Gardener reached over to the computer. "I'm going to show you some CCTV from the night in question, Mrs Challenger, the night your husband died."

Gardener started the recording. As he had already seen the clips a number of times, he chose instead to watch her reactions.

Once it had finished, he asked if she would like to see it again.

"No," said Grace, "I think I would like to contact my solicitor, now, please."

Chapter Forty-four

It was approaching early evening before Gardener and Reilly entered the interview room. Grace Challenger was present, with her solicitor, Belinda Scott, whose appearance suggested to Gardener they might have some trouble with her. Scott was possibly in her mid-fifties, with iron-grey hair tied up in a bun. She was slim, with a weathered face and glasses, and was dressed in a business suit that matched her hair. Prior to the interview, she had been with Grace for two hours.

Gardener went through the procedure for the recording equipment, and before he could actually say anything, Scott was on him.

"I'd like it noted how long my client has been held here, and that she has already been interviewed without me present."

Gardener glanced at Grace. "Have we been treating you well, Mrs Challenger?"

"I can't complain."

"Have you been fed, and given drinks?"

"Yes."

"Did you choose to speak to us without your solicitor earlier today, of your own free will?"

Grace's expression grew sheepish. "I suppose so, yes."

"Immaterial," said Scott. "You should have advised her she needed one. She's facing a murder charge."

Gardener continued to ignore Scott. "And are you happy to continue now, Mrs Challenger?"

"Certainly. The quicker we get this over with, the quicker I can go."

For Scott's sake, Gardener recapped on everything they had spoken about earlier, up to the point where Grace felt she had needed legal representation.

"I'd now like to turn my attention to the CCTV we showed you earlier, Mrs Challenger."

They ran it through twice, then Gardener said, "Are you happy that it is your car in the footage?"

"It looks like mine."

"You told us earlier that you had not left the house all evening?"

"Yes."

"How do you explain the car being where it is?"

"It's not up to my client to explain that," said Scott. "If she was at home all night, how could she know who had taken her car? You need to come up with better evidence than that, detective. Anyone could have been driving the car. Her husband for one."

"That's highly unlikely, isn't it?" said Reilly. "Even if her husband drove the car out to the agreed place, and someone else drove the van, he couldn't have driven it back on account of him being dead, now, could he?"

"I'd like some more proof before we continue with this conversation," said Scott.

"We thought you might say that, Belinda, love," said Reilly.

Scott bristled immediately. "Mrs Scott, to you."

"That does surprise me," said Reilly, icily.

Gardener took over, relishing the battle ahead between his partner and Grace's solicitor.

"Once we had seen the footage, we took the trouble of interviewing your client's closest neighbours. Anne Thompson lives on the right of Mrs Challenger and has a very good view of everyone who comes and goes. She saw Grace leave her house at seven forty-five on the night her husband was killed."

No comment was forthcoming so Gardener continued.

"When Mrs Thompson retired to bed at ten o'clock, Grace's house was still in darkness. The neighbour got up to go to the toilet at two o'clock, and your client's house was still in darkness, with no car on the drive, which is where it usually was."

"You're fishing, detective. This is not evidence," said Scott.

"Maybe this will help you," said Gardener. "Mrs Thompson did actually hear Grace's car pull on to the drive sometime around five o'clock in the morning. Glancing out the window she noticed Mrs Challenger approach her front door and fish around in her pocket for her keys. Mrs Thompson has signed a statement."

"Still proves nothing."

"Mrs Challenger," said Gardener. "Before I go any further, is there anything you would like to tell us?"

Scott shook her head. Grace declined to comment.

Gardener opened a manila folder and produced a series of blown-up photos.

"You wanted proof, Mrs Scott. You can have it. One of the houses on Haygate Lane has a rather top of the range digital CCTV system. Those cameras caught your client's car going past at three-thirty in the morning, and again at four-thirty, as you've already seen on the CCTV."

Gardener had had the photos enhanced. The clarity of the image was unquestionable. He passed them over.

"Would you agree Mrs Challenger that you are driving the car on both occasions?"

Grace's posture weakened. She opened her mouth to speak, but Belinda Scott put her off.

"I'd like to suspend the interview here and speak with my client in private."

"Oh, I can't do this anymore," said Grace. "There's no point."

"Do not say anything else until we've spoken," ordered Scott.

"Why?" said Grace. "You wanted evidence, and now you have it. That's me driving. They know it, I know it, and you know it. The game's up."

"Is that a confession?" asked Reilly.

Grace turned to her solicitor. "I know I asked you here, but it was only a matter of time. These boys are not stupid."

"I would still advise you to say nothing until we've spoken in private," said Scott, clearly unhappy.

"No," said Grace. "If I own up it might be better for me. They'll go easier."

A silence followed, and when it was obvious no one else was going to say anything, Gardener asked Grace if she'd like to tell everyone what had happened.

"I noticed things going wrong way back around December. He'd spent far too much time away from me; he'd been very secretive. Given that he was not the sharpest tool in the box, I found it very easy to see what he was up to. I discovered his infidelity through a Christmas present that turned out not to be mine. I saw them both in a garden centre. She was wearing the present that I thought had been meant for me.

"I started checking his phone and his computer equipment on a regular basis." Grace glanced upwards. "He was planning to leave me for her, you know, and they were actually considering setting up home in the Algarve – though Lord knows how he thought he could afford that, on a postman's salary.

"I couldn't let that happen. Following more research with his phone and laptop, I then discovered how he might have been able to afford such luxury in the Algarve. He was involved in a post office robbery with a bunch of low life criminals. That really shocked me. I had not been prepared for that one. I had to monitor him much more closely."

Grace started coughing and Gardener offered her some water. She accepted, and when the water was delivered and she'd taken a good drink, she continued.

"Davey had found out about the post office robberies from that low-life Frankie. He was shooting his mouth off in one of the local pubs, late one night and Davey had actually filmed a little of the conversation. Frankie, worse for wear, wasn't happy, and feeling sick of everything in general. He said that he took all the risks and Mitchell creamed off all the money, giving him a pittance. My husband listened, and he must have realized that Frankie and Mitchell were behind the recent post office jobs.

"He'd obviously given it some serious thought, because Davey then coerced Frankie into helping *him*, promising him a much better cut, leaving out Mitchell altogether. He persuaded Frankie that he could pull it off easily because *he* worked for the post office. They planned to use an old van of Mitchell's. Frankie and Mitchell would do what they always did, but Davey would muscle in at the last minute, and take the money. Once the heat had died down, Davey would drive the van into the field for Frankie to torch and, finally, arrange to meet him later to give him his share."

"Did you not feel a better course of action was to let your husband know what you knew, try to talk him out of it?" asked Gardener.

"Had it just been the robbery, I may have chosen that route."

Grace remained silent, but then continued with her confession.

"Once I was aware of the plan, and when it was happening, I followed Davey to the deserted barn, which was about a mile from the field where it was torched. Once he'd backed the van inside, he came out to lock the barn doors.

"I had already prepared the monkshood in a syringe. He went down very quickly. Writhed around, asked me what the hell I was doing. I told him I knew everything. He told me that it was all for us, and that I had made a mistake. Fat chance. He was even lying to me on his deathbed, so to speak. It was too late anyway. I dragged him back into the van and drove it to the field. I walked back to the barn, locked the doors and drove back home.

"Before I set off for home, I used Davey's phone to keep Frankie on side. I sent a text message - it's all yours. Frankie's job was to go into the field, remove everything that could identify it, and torch it. Looks like he couldn't even manage that."

"We don't know what went wrong, Mrs Challenger," said Gardener. "From the timing of everything, we can only surmise that Frankie got up late. He still managed to remove some of the identification and set fire to the van. Problem was, a jogger on Haygate Lane found it before it was fully burnt out. The fire brigade were called. I'm sure you can guess the rest."

There was nothing else anyone could say. The story was out, and like it or not, her solicitor had become redundant.

"Where's the money?" asked Reilly.

Following a lengthy silence, Grace finally said, "Well I'm afraid that remains an enigma. I have no idea what he's done with it. By the time he had brought the van to the barn and I had done what I needed to do, I searched van. There was no money."

Despite the missing cash being a problem, it wasn't really Gardener's. He would have to liaise with Tom Wilkinson and see what developed.

"What's going to happen to me?" asked Grace.

"I'm afraid it's not up to us, Mrs Challenger."

Gardener collected his paperwork and headed for the door.

Epilogue

Rebecca Adams, the clinic's director, was facing her computer monitor when the system pinged. Claire Fisher was passing the office. Rebecca called her in.

"We've just had clearance on a substantial amount of money to maintain Terry's fund."

"Oh, that's a relief," replied Claire, the senior nurse.

"Yes," said Rebecca. "It guarantees Terry's stay with us for at least another two years."

"As much as that? Oh my goodness."

"Were you about to go and see to Terry?" asked Rebecca.

"Yes, poor love," said Claire. "I've been a bit worried. We haven't seen his brother, Derrick, for a couple of days. I'm sure that Terry is missing him."

"He must have been busy, but he certainly hasn't forgotten him, has he?"

"Such a lovely man," said Claire. "Such dedication to his brother."

Claire left the office, walked down the corridor and opened Terry's door. The room had been cleaned, smelled fresh. The windows were open. He was sitting in an electronic frame that had been specifically designed to cater for all his needs during his waking hours, facing the windows, with a lovely view of the grounds, which included a large lake.

Claire crossed the room to face Terry. Gazing at him she felt so saddened by his blank expression. She couldn't even begin to know what he was thinking, if anything. To be so full of life one minute, and then to slowly lose it all. But at least he had everything he needed here. And who knows, however slim his chances, he may recover enough to lead something of a life.

"Hello, Terry, love. How are you?"

Terry blinked. Perhaps he understood some things.

"We've just heard from Derrick. I think he's been really busy, but I'm sure he will be along to see you soon."

Terry's expression remained blank. He did not blink, but a tear left his eye.

If you enjoyed this book, please let others know by leaving a quick review on Amazon. Also, if you spot anything untoward in the paperback, get in touch. We strive for the best quality and appreciate reader feedback.

editor@thebookfolks.com

www.thebookfolks.com

ALSO AVAILABLE

If you enjoyed IMPLICATION, the ninth book, check out the others in the series:

IMPURITY – *Book 1*

Someone is out for revenge. A grotto worker is murdered in the lead up to Christmas. He won't be the first. Can DI Gardener stop the killer, or is he saving his biggest gift till last?

IMPERFECTION – *Book 2*

When theatre-goers are treated to the gruesome spectacle of an actor's lifeless body hanging on the stage, DI Stewart Gardener is called in to investigate. Is the killer still in the audience? A lockdown is set in motion but it is soon apparent that the murderer is able to come and go unnoticed. Identifying and capturing the culprit will mean establishing the motive for their crimes, but perhaps not before more victims meet their fate.

IMPLANT – *Book 3*

A small Yorkshire town is beset by a series of cruel murders. The victims are tortured in bizarre ways. The killer leaves a message with each crime – a playing card from an obscure board game. DI Gardener launches a manhunt but it will only be by figuring out the murderer's motive that they can bring him to justice.

IMPRESSION – *Book 4*

Police are stumped by the case of a missing five-year-old girl until her photograph turns up under the body of a murdered woman. It is the first lead they have and is quickly followed by the discovery of another body connected to the case. Can DI Stewart Gardener find the connection between the individuals before the abducted child becomes another statistic?

IMPOSITION – *Book 5*

When a woman's battered body is reported to police by her husband, it looks like a bungled robbery. But the investigation begins to turn up disturbing links with past crimes. They are dealing with a killer who is expert at concealing his identity. Will they get to him before a vigilante set on revenge?

IMPOSTURE – *Book 6*

When a hit and run claims the lives of two people, DI Gardener begins to realize it was not a random incident. But when he begins to track down the elusive suspects he discovers that a vigilante is getting to them first. Can the detective work out the mystery before more lives are lost?

IMPASSIVE – *Book 7*

A publisher racked with debts is found strung up in a ruined Yorkshire abbey. Has a disgruntled author taken their revenge? DI Stewart Gardener is on the case but maybe a hypnotist has the key to the puzzle. Can the cop muster his team to work some magic and catch a cunning killer?

IMPIOUS – *Book 8*

It could be detectives Gardener and Reilly's most disturbing case yet when a body with head, limbs and torso assembled from different victims is discovered. Alongside this grotesque being is a cryptic message and a chess piece. A killer wants to take the cops on a journey. And force their hand.

Other titles of interest

OUT FOR REVENGE by Tony Bassett

When a dangerous prisoner is released he has plans to up his drugs business. But someone will quickly put an end to that, by putting an end to his life. Detective Sunita Roy has the unenviable task of hunting down the gangsters who were likely responsible. But when the cops close in, they'll have an even bigger problem than they first imagined.

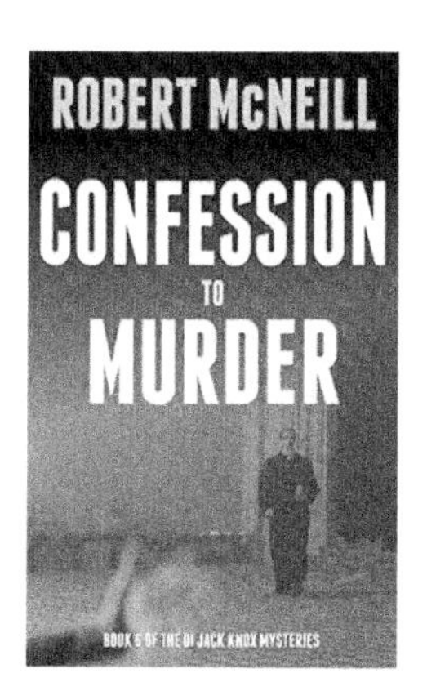

CONFESSION TO MURDER by Robert McNeill

After a man confesses in church that he has killed a girl, having wrangled with his conscience the priest tells the police. It would be easy for them to dismiss the confessor as a crank, but DI Knox has a hunch the victim could be a young Canadian tourist who has gone missing. Yet with few other leads, it will take brilliant detective work to catch the killer.

All FREE with Kindle Unlimited and available in paperback!

www.thebookfolks.com

Printed in Great Britain
by Amazon